COLTRANE'S
JOURNEY

COLTRANE'S JOURNEY

•

Danny C. Thornsberry

AVALON BOOKS
NEW YORK

PRINTED IN THE UNITED STATES OF AMERICA
ON ACID-FREE PAPER
BY HADDON CRAFTSMEN, BLOOMSBURG, PENNSYLVANIA

To old Moe

CONTENTS

Chapter One
The Escape

I don't suppose death surprised me very much anymore. It had been too frequent a visitor during my short life for me not to be expecting it to show up sooner or later. Five years earlier it had taken my mother and two days ago it had visited my father in the form of a fever.

Death had left me alone to scratch out a living on a hardscrabble Eastern Kentucky farm. It was a cruel turn of events for a seventeen-year-old-boy brought up on tall tales of mountain men, Indian fighters, and cowboys.

It was cruel in the sense that when I compared the life I was going to live staring at the south end of a mule pulling a plow all day long to the lives lived by the likes of a Jim Bridger or a Kit Carson, my life didn't even come in at second place.

And with each passing day I grew more desperate to escape. But a lack of money bound me to that forty acres of dirt as surely as if I'd been shackled in a jail cell somewhere.

Of course I'd thought of trying to sell the place, but there were few people willing to buy it. And those who could

buy the farm wouldn't want to pay anywhere near what it
was worth. For times were hard in the hills—with the value
of a silver dollar growing faster than anything that was ever
planted in the poor soil of a hillside farm.

And if there was one thing I'd learned over the years,
there was no substitute for cash money. Even a man as
independent as a prospector needed a grubstake to tide him
over until he could find one of those creeks peppered with
gold nuggets the size of hen's eggs I'd been hearing about.

I didn't know how much of a stake I'd need to get me
to Texas, but I sure knew how much the outfit I'd be needing when I got there would cost. For I'd sure given the
matter plenty of thought while lying awake in my bed at
night. The best I could figure, a saddle, horse, and weapons
would run me around a hundred and fifty dollars.

I was a long way from having that kind of money. My
entire fortune consisted of twenty silver dollars earned running a trapline and working for other folks when I could
spare the time away from Pa's farm. And with what appeared to be another bad year for crops shaping up, I knew
I wouldn't be adding any more silver dollars to the poke I
kept hidden in the chimney of the cabin.

So while my heart and soul were in Texas, the lack of
money was keeping my body in Kentucky. And barring
some sort of a miracle, it appeared I'd be staying in the
Bluegrass state.

And on the mile-long walk back to my log house, frus-
tration and worry about the situation kept me company and
distracted me to the point where I'd walked to within fifty
feet of the cabin before I noticed that the door was open
and that there was smoke coming from the chimney. A few
seconds later, I smelled the aroma of roasting meat coming
from inside the cabin.

Somebody had broken into my home and was cooking

himself something to eat—pretty nervy for a county where more than one man had been shot for trespassing.

I was just wrapping my mind around that last thought when I noticed the chicken feathers at my feet. "Well, that tears it," I muttered to myself. Laying hens were hard enough to come by as it was without letting some chicken-thief make a meal out of one of the few I'd managed to keep the foxes and weasels from getting.

Tossing the shovel I was carrying aside, I sprinted for the door, intent on throwing the chicken-thief inside my house out on his ear.

Bursting through the door with clenched fists, I ended up staring into the mean, bloodshot eyes of Tory Riley—a fat, bearded man whose name was the first one mentioned when stolen property was trying to be located, and the last person anyone wanted to see around his home place. But here he was, sitting at my table in one of the cabin's two chairs. And if that wasn't bad enough, he'd brought along his two no-good brothers, Ollie and Rafe.

With none of the Rileys standing less than six feet tall and weighing less than two hundred pounds, I knew that my original plan to throw out whoever had broken into my home was going to have to be amended. In fact, I knew I would have to watch my step or I could end up being thumped.

But I was at an age when good judgment was sometimes hard to throw a loop on. And besides, the Coltrane farm was now mine and I had a responsibility to look out for it. So when I saw my chicken roasting on the spit in the fireplace, that was the last straw. Throwing all caution and good sense to the wind, I let them know how things stood.

Turning to face Tory with my fists still firmly clenched, I said, "Riley, when my pa was alive you and your sorry kin were never invited over here, and I don't intend to start asking you over now. So git!"

Well, I'd done flung-the-chunk, and I was expecting to be throwing some punches and taking my lumps, but not one of them had made a move. Tory, the eldest and leader of the clan, only smiled at the insult.

He obviously didn't consider me to be much of a threat. Not that he had any reason to believe that I was, for after all, I wasn't anything but another skinny mountain boy dressed in a buckskin shirt and a pair of linsey-woolsey pants that had been patched so many times it was hard to tell where the patches left off and the original material took up.

But even though I was just a kid, they apparently weren't planning on taking any chances with me. I noticed that Ollie had moved behind me and was nervously fingering the bone handle of the foot-long Bowie knife he carried in the sheath on his belt.

Rafe, the third brother, was to my right cradling a double-barreled shotgun in the crook in his arm. I didn't know what they were up to, but it seemed as if it was more than their usual thieving and bullying they'd become so well known for. Whatever they had planned, I figured I wasn't going to like it. And I couldn't help but feel that I'd walked into some kind of a trap.

Reaching inside his coat pocket, Tory pulled out what looked to be some sort of official document.

Continuing to smile—a smile that was really beginning to annoy me—he said, "It may come as something of a shock to you, boy, but every now and then your pa liked to tie one on, and when the whiskey started to get to him he liked to play poker. The last time he played, he lost this here farm."

Leaning forward, Tory placed the paper he'd taken from

his pocket on the table and pushed it over to where I stood. Clearing his throat, Tory said, "I'm the man who won it. That there's the deed to this place—made out to me all legal and proper."

Glancing down at the document, I could see where someone had made his mark and where my father's name, Amos Coltrane, had been printed out beside it. And right below his supposed signature were the signatures of two witnesses. I couldn't say that I was surprised to see that the names of the witnesses were Ollie and Rafe Riley.

It was obvious that the deed was as phony as a three-dollar bill, and I had no doubt that it could be proved in court that it was a fake. But by the time I could take the place back it would be picked as clean as the chicken roasting on the spit in the fireplace. I knew right then that if I planned to save the farm I had to put the Rileys off the place before they had a chance to strip it clean.

Out of the corner of my eye I could see that Ollie's big knife was still in its scabbard, so I leaned over the table until I was almost nose-to-nose with Tory and said, "I've only got one thing to say about that deed, Tory."

"What's that?" he asked.

"It's as worthless as you and your whole low-down family!"

That surprised him enough to give me a chance to reach around and grab a handful of greasy hair and bring his face down hard on the tabletop, splintering wood and breaking bones.

Knowing that Rafe would be slow to bring the long-barreled shotgun into action within the confines of the small room, I wheeled around to face Ollie, who by that time had pulled his knife and was getting ready to skewer me with it. But I was much quicker and more agile than the heavyset renegade, so when I leaned back to avoid his thrust, the razor-sharp blade missed my chest by at least two inches.

Ollie was big and powerful, but he was slow; his right foot was still extended from the thrust he'd made. Seeing my chance, I came down hard on the extended foot with my heavy workboot.

I'd put all my weight behind the blow and since I weighed around a hundred and sixty pounds, I wasn't surprised to hear the bones crack in Ollie's extended foot and see him drop to the floor screaming in pain.

Swinging to the left to engage Rafe, my chin met the butt of his shotgun first, causing me to fall to the floor wondering why the stars were out in the middle of the afternoon.

Fighting hard to regain consciousness, I became dimly aware of Rafe trying to swing the shotgun like some sort of a club, but the ceiling was too low and the walls too close together to let him put enough force behind the blows to do any real damage.

Giving up in disgust, he started kicking me in the ribs; tiring of that, he eared back the hammers of the shotgun and started to back up hoping to put the barrels of the gun against my chest and pull the triggers.

But the pain from being kicked in the ribs had roused me enough to where I was able to reach up and wrap my arm around the barrels of the shotgun and hold on for dear life.

Rafe tried his best to shake me loose. He dragged me floundering all over the room where I ended up bumping into everything in it at least once until I was finally dragged to where Ollie had dropped his knife. Grasping the weapon with my free hand, I looked up at Rafe. And seeing that I was now armed, Rafe panicked.

In his rush to get away he dropped the shotgun and

leaped for the door but got tangled up in his own feet and
fell out into the yard where I caught up to him and rapped
him upside the head with the heavy wood-and-brass handle
of the Bowie knife. This resulted in him losing a couple of
teeth and dropping to the ground like he'd been poleaxed.
Later Rafe would lay claim to being the luckiest of his
brothers in that he'd only lost a couple of teeth and got a
few bruises in the fracas. His brothers, nursing their broken
bones, were quick to agree with his opinion.

It was hard work dragging out the heavy bodies of Ollie
and Tory from inside of my cabin, so I was ready to rest
up a mite, and when I sat on the porch to take my well-
earned break, I also used the opportunity to take a closer
look at the deed Tory had shown me.

There was no doubt in my mind that the document was
a forgery, but I knew enough about the law to know that
the Rileys could find themselves some lawyer who'd be
willing to drag the whole thing through court until he'd
gotten every penny he could from them, and that I, to keep
from getting run over in court by their lawyer, would have
to hire an attorney of my own. It wasn't all that hard to
raise a stink in the county legal system—all it took was a
few dollars to start the paperwork.

I didn't know what to do. I'd just lost my pa; my dream
of becoming a Texas cowpuncher was pretty much over;
and now I was in a battle to keep what little property I
owned, getting ready to fight some lawyer in court. If I'd
been a little less stubborn—and a whole lot smarter—I
would have been packing up and hitting the trail about then.

Such were my thoughts when I heard the hoofbeats on
the road below my cabin. Looking down the hill I recognized the big red mule of Lemuel Jones, my nearest neigh-
bor and the county sheriff.

Riding up to the front of my cabin, he looked down at

the sprawled and unconscious bodies of the Rileys laid out in front of it.

Crossing his right leg around the saddle horn, Jones polished the badge pinned to his bib overalls with his shirt sleeve.

"Howdy, Matt," he said. "Couldn't help but notice that you got all the Riley boys laid out here all nice and peaceful-like. You got some reason for that?"

Taking the deed out of my pocket, I handed it up to him and said, "They showed up here with this and tried to run me off the place."

Fishing out his spectacles, he put them on and began to read the paper. He paused several times to peer over the glasses at the Rileys who were beginning to stir. After he'd finished reading the document, he folded it and put it in one of the bib overalls' many pockets—he often referred to his overalls as a country boy's filing cabinet.

Staring at Rafe who seemed to be the least disabled at the time and would probably be the one who could answer a few questions, Jones asked, "Which one of you old boys came up with the idea of trying to steal Amos Coltrane's farm?"

Mad from having been bested by a mere boy, Rafe protested, "What are you saying, Sheriff? That there's a legal deed—we own this here farm."

"That a fact?" asked Jones.

"Durn right!" said Rafe.

Removing the spectacles, the sheriff put them back in his case and said, "Just how is it that you boys ended up with this deed anyway?"

Fearing some sort of trap, Rafe took a few seconds to think before he answered. "Matt's pa got drunk one night and lost it to Tory in a card game."

Jones's eyes narrowed—they always did that when he thought he heard a lie.

"I also noticed that the names of the men who witnessed Amos Coltrane's mark on that deed were you and Ollie. What about it, Rafe, you and Ollie sign your names to that deed?" asked Jones.

"Yep, sure did," answered Rafe.

The scowl that had been on the sheriff's face was gone and in its place there was a broad grin and he began to laugh.

Knowing that the sheriff had somehow tripped him up in his story, Rafe became indignant. Rising to his full height, Rafe said, "I'll have you know that every word I spoke is pure gospel."

Chuckling, the sheriff said, "If I were you, Rafe, I'd make durn sure I wasn't standing out in the rain when I talked like that—for a bolt of lightning might just come down from the sky and fry your lying hide."

Rafe really hated doing it, but he couldn't keep from looking skyward to see if any clouds were gathering.

Seeing that the other Rileys had come to, the sheriff spoke to all of them. "Since I've had dealings with you boys before, I know that trying to get the truth out of you is like trying to herd a bunch of cats. So I'll just tell you how I know that deed is a fake."

Taking a few seconds to get his thoughts in order, Jones explained, "To begin with, Amos Coltrane was a teetotaler. He never touched the stuff. Secondly, he couldn't abide gambling in any form. He wouldn't even flip a coin to help him decide what road to take—let alone bet his home on the turn of a card."

Jones paused to let what he'd said sink in. And when the importance of what had been said began to dawn on Tory, he asked, "What about the deed? You got Coltrane's mark on that."

"I'm glad you brought that up, Tory," replied Jones. "Amos Coltrane was a mighty educated man for these parts. He could not only read and write but could do it well enough to be able to teach young Matt here how to do the same. So why should a man who could sign his name make a mark on something as important as a deed?"

Tory was probably thinking of suggesting that Amos had made his mark because he'd been too drunk to sign his name, but then he remembered that Jones had pretty much ruled out the possibility of Coltrane being drunk.

"Something else about that deed I find peculiar is the fact that the two witnesses to Amos's signature were Ollie and Rafe. How is it that two men who've never been known to sign their names to anything before all of a sudden put their signatures to a deed? And in what I might add appears to be a mighty fine hand."

Seeing that Tory was about to protest, the sheriff held up his hand and said, "Before you dig that hole you're standing in any deeper, Tory, I think you should know we can have your brothers sign their names right now and see how they stack up against the signatures on that deed."

Tory could see that he was caught; he knew his brothers couldn't even begin to sign their names—he'd hired a man to draw up the deed and sign his brother's names to it. It had seemed like a pretty slick idea at the time. But now he could see how poorly the whole thing had been thought out.

When Tory had first heard about Amos Coltrane being at death's door he figured getting a fake deed and moving in would be a piece of cake, especially with the only thing standing in his way being a wet-behind-the-ears kid. He had no idea that I could be as tough as shoe leather; he also didn't figure on the sheriff sticking his nose in the dispute.

Hoping to retain at least a bit of his dignity, Tory addressed Jones. "Okay, Sheriff, I don't see it the way you do, but me and my brothers got better things to do than to stand around here all day arguing over this little patch of dirt. So we'll just be on our way."

Then, shaking his fist at me, he said, "I'll not be forgettin' what you did to me and my kin, boy. I'll be a-seein' you somewhere down the trail."

Losing his patience, the sheriff unhooked his leg from around the saddle horn and dropped to the ground. Grabbing Tory by the collar with one hand, Jones pulled him to his feet and said, "You and your brothers have been a thorn in my side for long enough, Tory. And you've given this boy all the grief you're going to."

Rising to his full height after the sheriff released his collar, Tory tried very hard to look dignified. He dearly wanted to say something to Jones to ease his wounded pride, but he knew better than to push the county sheriff too far, for he was a very tough man who pushed back—hard.

There was no way Tory figured on bracing the big man since he was not only half a foot taller and fifty pounds heavier than himself, but a well-known rough-and-tumble fighter. It was also a fact that Jones carried other things in his pockets besides papers and spectacles—some of which were downright lethal.

"Think you can learn to live with it, Tory" asked the sheriff.

Looking puzzled, Tory asked, "Live with what?"

"Ain't it occured to you what it's going to be like when word gets out about how the three of you set out to run some orphan kid off his place and ended up getting your heads handed to you by that same kid? Why, it's hard for me to keep from laughing every time I think about it."

Tory and Rafe's shoulders sagged. They knew the sheriff was right; they'd be lucky if they could walk down the street in town without kids throwing rocks at them once word got out about what had happened.

Rafe most likely was wondering if it would be mentioned that they had been armed while I didn't have any kind of a weapon on me. Folks would definitely mention it since that made the story even funnier.

The only one of the brothers who wasn't concerned about what people would say was Ollie—he was in so much pain because of his broken foot he didn't care whether or not somebody wanted to call him a blue-eyed milk cow as long as they'd do something for his injured foot.

"If it was me, Tory I'd be making plans to find somewhere else to hang my hat. And given what you boys are going to be trying to live down, I'd make it as far away from here as I could get."

Without saying a word, Tory nodded to Rafe and they helped their brother to his feet. Actually it would be more accurate to say they helped him to his foot since it would be some time due to the pain before Ollie could put any weight on his injured foot.

Supporting their wounded brother between them, the Rileys hobbled on down the road. Tory knew of a place in the next county where some horses could be stolen and a root cellar plundered before they headed for safer—and less embarrassing—parts.

"Well, there they go: the broken, the bruised, and the cut. Do you think anybody around here will be missing them?" asked Jones, as he extended his hand to me.

"Nobody I can think of," I replied, taking the offered hand.

"I doubt even their mother would miss them," added Jones.

Remembering my manners, I said, "If you have the time, Sheriff, I can put on some coffee." And as an afterthought I added, "And offer you some roasted chicken."

Jones's eyes lit up. "Well, it ain't Sunday, but I don't have no objections to sittin' down to a Sunday chicken dinner even if it ain't the Sabbath."

Leading the way back into the cabin, I threw together a makeshift table and put together a meal of baked potatoes that the Rileys had been cooking under the hot coals of the fireplace, and, unhappily, one of my few—and highly-prized—laying hens.

Fortunately, both of the chairs had remained undamaged so the sheriff and I could sit at the table in comfort.

"I'm sure glad you showed up when you did, Sheriff. I really didn't know how to go about handling the Rileys."

Taking a sip of hot coffee, Jones smiled and said, "The way things looked when I rode up here, I'd say you knew exactly how to to handle them."

"I just got lucky," I said.

Chuckling, the sheriff said, "Luck you say. Well, I guess there was some luck involved in that fight. But the luck was with the Rileys—not you."

"How you figure that?" I asked.

"Those old boys were lucky you didn't kill them," he said, guffawing.

After he stopped laughing, Jones turned serious and asked, "I would like to know what made you tackle that bunch by yourself instead of coming to me for help."

"Not enough time. I figured that by the time I could get them off the place it would have been stripped clean."

"You're probably right," he agreed, pushing back from the table. "They would have cleaned you out in no time at all."

Walking back outside, we both took seats on the porch.

Jones was staring toward the distant hills when he spoke. "What are your plans now that your pa's passed on, Matt?"

"Work the farm like always, I reckon," I said, leaning against a post.

"Have you given up on the idea of heading West?"

"No choice in the matter since I don't have an outfit or enough money to tide me over until I can find work, and nobody around here has the money to buy me out."

Knocking the ashes out of his pipe on the edge of the porch, Jones asked, "What do you figure this place is worth?"

Thinking for a few seconds I answered, "About two hundred dollars with the tools and livestock."

"Sounds about right," he agreed.

Sitting in silence for a couple of minutes, the sheriff cleared his throat before he spoke. "Now Matt, it's not that I'm being nosy or anything like that, but have you managed to put away any money?"

"About twenty dollars," I answered.

"Seems that I recall you telling me one time that a horse, saddle, and weapons would cost you about a hundred and fifty dollars. Is that right?"

"Yes," I answered, knowing the sheriff was trying to make some sort of a point—but I didn't have a clue as to what it might be.

"Matt, did you know that the big cattle outfits out West supply their riders with mounts?"

"No," I answered. I still didn't know what he has driving at with his questions—but he certainly had my attention.

"I figure that fifty dollars would buy you that Winchester

rifle you've been talking about and a pretty good saddle—
not to mention the fact that you'd have enough of a grubstake left over to keep you in beans for quite some time."

"I reckon you're right, Mr. Jones, but I'm still thirty
short of that fifty dollars, with the only thing I have to sell
being this farm. And with so few folks around here with
ready cash, selling this place don't seem likely."

"I agree," said Jones. "Finding somebody around here
with two hundred dollars hard cash is next to impossible.
But finding somebody with fifty dollars who'd be willing
to part with it as a down payment on this farm is possible."

Turning to me, Jones asked, "If such a man could be
found, would you be willing to sell him your farm on those
terms?"

"In a heartbeat," I answered.

"Well, you're looking at that man. I'm interested in your
place. Or I should say my eldest is interested in your place.
You see, he's about to get married and needs a place to
farm."

I was stunned. I couldn't believe how fast things had
changed. This morning I was chained to the land; now I
was as free as a bird—I barely listened to the sheriff as he
explained the arrangements.

"Tommorow morning you show up at the courthouse and
I'll have Judge Tiner draw up the contract. The way I figure
it, my son will pay you fifty dollars down and make pay-
ments of twenty-five dollars a year, due on the same date,
for the next six years. That suit you, Matt?"

Still in something of a trance, I nodded my agreement.

Taking the hand Jones offered to seal the deal, I shook
it.

"Done, then!" said Jones, as he pumped my arm.

"I suppose I made a better deal than I'd planned on making," he said.

"How's that?" I asked.

"Well, when word gets out about the Rileys leaving the county, property values are bound to go up."

We both laughed.

Chapter Two
Riding the River

The contract was drawn up, the papers signed, and all business finished in less than two hours. Jones's son was now tied to the farm and I was a free man with money in my pocket—actually it was in a money belt strapped to my waist.

I was also finding out that having a bit of money had a tendency to make your life more complicated. For I had to open a bank account so that the yearly mortage payment could be deposited and properly recorded. Judge Tiner also suggested that I make out a will. When I pointed out that I had no known living relatives, he allowed as how he'd never known of a healthy young man who didn't end up with relatives sooner or later. I agreed as to the possibility of such an occurrence and signed my name to the document with the provision of naming a beneficiary at a later date.

I also came into five dollars I hadn't been expecting. The sheriff had confiscated Rafe's shotgun and Ollie's knife, auctioned them off on the courthouse steps, and given me the proceeds—saying for me to think of the money as the Rileys' way of apologizing for their rude behavior during their visit.

Jones also pointed out that the bids he'd received for the weapons were the highest he'd ever seen. The word about what had happened out at my place was starting to spread and folks wanted to see what kind of armament the Rileys had been packing when they got their butts kicked by the skinny orphan kid.

With the security of a money belt strapped to my waist, and knowing I wouldn't have to be on the lookout for the Rileys, I headed out of town for Ezra Jensen's poultry farm. About twice a year Jensen drove a large flock of geese to market on the Maysville Road. He usually hired around ten young boys who he paid a nickel a day to act as drovers herding the fowl to the town of Maysville on the Ohio River. With roads being what they were in Kentucky in the 1880s, it was the cheapest way to get them the sixty miles to market. And Jensen was well known for his ability to hold on to a dollar.

I had made that drive myself when I was younger and I knew it was quite a job keeping all those geese headed in one direction and not letting them get into folks' crops who lived along the right-of-way. And that didn't even take into account keeping dogs, varmints, and other critters from trying to grab themselves a free goose dinner every now and then. Although that wasn't half as hard as keeping the two-legged type of varmints, such as the Rileys, from trying for a free meal.

I hadn't actually been looking for a job as one of the drovers. What I had in mind was being hired as sort of the drive's hunter. Given that it took several days to reach Maysville, Jensen had to spend money for grub. And ten hungry, growing boys, their appetites whetted by walking all day, could take a sizeable chunk out of his profits.

It was pretty hard to bargain with the wiry old man. I even had the feeling that if I hadn't been on my toes during the negotiations, I could have ended up paying him for just traveling with them. But finally a deal was struck. It was decided that instead of being one of the drovers I would spend all my time hunting. And Jensen made sure that I would earn my money, for he only carried salt and a few seasonings in his pack. If I failed to find game along the trail, it would be a hungry camp I would be sleeping in. And I sure didn't want to listen to the complaints of a bunch of hungry kids.

We were on the second day of the drive and I was just returning from my day's hunt. Looking up from the cook-fire he had just made, Jensen spotted me. " 'Bout time you was gettin' here, Coltrane. What kind of varmint you shoot for the pot tonight? Possum or coon?"

"Neither, Mr. Jensen," I replied, removing the game bag slung around my shoulder.

"Pretty much a mixed bag. Three rabbits, a squirrel, and a turkey," I said, upending the bag and pouring them out onto the ground.

I knew that Jensen had only been kidding. He knew full well that I wouldn't be throwing lead from that old .32 caliber muzzle-loader at a possom or a coon. Especially since he was footing the bill for my powder and shot, he would have throwed a fit if I had wasted a lead ball on such table fare. I still remembered the ruckus he raised when I shot a hawk that was swooping down on one of his geese the day before. I'd been downright proud of hitting that fast-moving predator on the wing. But the way Jensen carried on about how much lead and powder cost and there I was wasting it on something even the dogs would turn their noses up at, you would have thought I had hit the darn goose instead of the hawk.

In general, the boys and I suffered because of Jensen's miserly ways, but on occasion we benefited from them.

Because of his frugality, Jensen did all of the preparation and cooking of the food. He let nothing go to waste and used seasoning and spices to stretch whatever was left over in a pot or pan into another meal. But it was these very methods that caused him to add flavors to the food that made all of us come back for seconds and sometimes thirds. I don't think Jensen ever figured out what had happened or he would have opened up a restaurant somewhere and gotten rich.

After supper we'd gather around the campfire. The talk was pleasant at night. Hard work and a full belly had a tendency to relax you whether you were man or boy. But while the talk was pleasant, it was short. For the boys were tired and it wasn't long before they had all crawled off to their bed rolls.

I always laid my bed roll at the edge of camp where I would be nearer the geese if some varmint decided to raid the flock. This was one of my jobs. Since Jensen and I were the only ones who were armed, we each stood a turn at guard duty.

Leaning against an oak tree, I laid the rifle in my lap. I knew I could get some sleep without worrying, for if something stirred among the geese, Jensen's herd dogs would set off the alarm.

Sitting there, I had time to reflect on how things were working out. Right now, I was heading north and not the direction I had been planning. I only took the job because it was a chance to make some money to add to my money belt. Jensen was paying me two dollars. And I was eating for free. And since I had sold the farm, I no longer had a home. So I might as well stay on the move. Especially when I could get paid for it and eat for free.

On occasion I would touch the money belt to reassure myself that it was still there. I jealously guarded each and every one of those dollars. The only time I planned to go into that belt was when I found a Winchester model '73 in caliber 44-40. I could see the weapon in my mind's eye. And I eased on off into sleep with that thought.

Jensen raised quite a fuss about paying me the full amount for hunting when he found out I wouldn't be returning home with him and would therefore not be shooting game for their camps at night. He was pretty stubborn about the whole matter until I showed him the buck I had shot that morning. He and the boys would have more than enough meat to do them on the way back home. After thinking things over, he finally relented. I knew he was aware that I could have sold the venison and hide of that deer in Maysville for twice what he was paying me. In addition he would have to buy grub at city prices, to feed everybody for at least three days on the trail.

In the end, for the most part, we parted company in a friendly manner.

All things considered, the trip had been a pleasant walk in the country, and profitable for everyone involved. And it was during that stroll I began to wonder if this method of traveling where I could make money by selling wild game to people as I went along couldn't be repeated. Maybe all the way to Texas. Anyway, Maysville was a pretty big town, and would be a good place to find out if my idea would work.

I was beginning to wonder if my plan to pay my way selling wild game to people in settlements was going to pan out. I'd been walking the streets of Maysville for two hours without success when I stepped into a tavern to try my luck once again.

The owner was a heavyset man named Fredric York, who was far from encouraging.

"Got no need for a hunter. Got enough good-for-nothin' relatives who spend all their time in the woods huntin' and makin' whiskey as it is. They keep me well supplied with meat and likker," he said as he wiped down the bar with a rag.

"Thanks anyway," I said. And turned to leave.

I was pulled up short by a booming voice coming from the back of the room. "Hold it there, boy!"

I turned to see a giant of a man sitting at a far table. Motioning for me to join him, he kicked a chair out from under the table. "Sit down, boy," he said, pointing to the chair.

Ordinarily I would have been put off by such behavior, and being young and full of vinegar I was inclined to buck the odds when it came to a fight. But there was something about this man that demanded respect. It wasn't just the fact that he weighed around three hundred pounds, but the many scars that covered his face and bulging arms let me know that this was a man who had fought more than a few battles. And the fact that he was still here told me that he was good at brawling.

"My name's John Rink, boy," he said. "Did I hear you say you was trying to find work as a meat hunter?"

"That's right."

"Well, it just so happens that I'm in need of a hunter." Then, seeming to notice my youth and shoulders that hadn't quite filled out yet, he said, "But I need one who can take care of himself and not be afraid of the boogeyman when it gets dark." Looking me over more closely, he asked, "Just how old are you, boy?"

"I'm seventeen, mister. And I ain't afraid of no boogeyman. Or any man for that matter. Including you."

Well, you would have thought that I had just slapped that man right across the mouth. Jerking upright in his chair, his jaw dropped open in surprise. But the surprise didn't last long, for his jaw set and his eyes leveled on me. The cold, hard look he gave me made me pause to reconsider my rash words and made me wish I had been born a mute.

I don't mind saying that I was almighty uncomfortable standing there holding his gaze. But I stood there anyway. And it was with great relief that I saw a smile begin across his face.

"Salty, ain't you, boy? I reckon you'll do to ride the river with. Have a seat, mister, and let's talk it over," Rink said, motioning toward the chair.

It was the first opportunity I had to talk myself into a job, and I intended to make the most of it.

"Mr. Rink, my name is Matthew Coltrane. I hail from sixty miles south of here. Now, I know I'm young, but I've got experience hunting. I've been tramping through the woods since I was big enough to pack this old rifle around. And don't be fooled by the way this old piece looks," I said, patting the stock of the old rifle. "She's been banged around a bit but she's been well taken care of and shoots truer than most men talk."

Pulling a cigar from his vest picket, Rink lit it and watched the smoke rise to the ceiling.

"Mr. Coltrane, I have five flatboats filled with people, their livestock, and goods. We plan on floating on down the Mississippi River to New Orleans. Several of these people have relatives down there who are going to help them start a new life." Pausing, he knocked the ashes from his cigar.

"As you know, times have been tough around here. And these people have paid me to see them safe to New Orleans. Unfortunately, they can't be dipping into their own stores to feed my crew, or even themselves for that matter. So we need to add to our grub from the woods as much as possible." Pausing again, he allowed me to think about the situation.

"Now, I need every one of my crew to handle the boats and can't afford to let them hunt for food. So what it comes down to is that you will have to supply enough wild meat to feed over forty people every day. That's your part. My part of the bargain is that I will pay you twenty-five cents for every day you hunt. Which will be every day that we are on the river. I'll supply the ammunition, of course. And you will also get to share in our stores of coffee, sugar, beans, and other staples."

Pointing to the possibles bag slung around my shoulder, Rink said, "It don't appear that you carry much in the way of such civilized grub on your person."

He was right about that, for I was a man who traveled light. Most of the stuff I carried in my bag was there to keep my gun in good repair, and start cook fires. I looked forward to night camps where I could eat beans and drink real coffee.

Seeing that I was eager to take the job, Rink cautioned me, "Now, son, this ain't going to be no walk down a country lane. You need to consider that there will be danger on this trip. There's still hazards aplenty along the river. And not all of the dangers come from the river itself or wild animals. I've been a riverman a good part of my life, and I've fought everything from pirates to bears. And I have no doubt that we will be in more than one scrape before this trip is over. So, you need to think hard about whether or not you want to sign on with us."

Standing, I stuck out my hand. "Mr. Rink, you just hired yourself a hunter."

Smiling, he took my hand and shook it. "Good! Let's get started."

As he stood, I could see that I had misjudged his size. He weighed close to three hundred pounds all right, but he stood over six feet tall, so little if any of the weight was fat. And on his left side, in cross-draw fashion, he carried an ivory-gripped Colt .45. It was one of the seven-and-one-half-inch models supplied to the U.S. Cavalry. On his right side he carried a foot-long Bowie knife. It looked similar to the one that Ollie Riley had carried, but I was sure that John Rink could handle his knife with much more skill.

Walking down to the river, we stopped at what I took to be the lead boat. Nearby were four other flatboats with people milling about caring for livestock and generally going about their business. I assumed that these were the people I would be feeding.

John Rink spoke to a man on the boat, who quickly disappeared into the boat's hold for a few minutes. Returning, he handed Rink a large sack. Rink then struck out upriver, motioning for me to follow. Stopping by a canoe, he handed me the sack.

"There's some supplies in that poke you will need until we rendezvous," he said, as he took out his pocket watch. "It's mid-morning. I want you to get in this canoe and float on down the river till dark. Make camp and spend the next day hunting. We should join you in about two days. If we're not there in three days, we won't be coming. In that case, the canoe and supplies are yours."

I didn't know what he meant by that, but it did sound downright mysterious. But it wasn't my place to question my new boss, so I just said, "Yes sir," and launched the canoe.

After floating on the river for about an hour, my curiosity got the better of me and I opened the sack. I tell you I was as happy as a kid on Christmas morning. I found a frying pan, a cooking pot, flour, cornmeal, salt, sugar, beans, and coffee. Wrapped up separately was a powder flask and an ingot of lead.

I could have lived like a king for months with all of those supplies. And then I remembered what Rink had said about the possibility of his not showing up.

The sun was straight up when I pulled the canoe over to a shaded island. I had a real hankering to sample some of the goods in the sack. Building a small fire, I put on the coffee. While waiting for it to boil, I cut a green willow over which I curled some of the flour I had mixed with water to form a thick dough. Twirling the dough around the stick, I heated it over the fire until it turned a nice brown.

Sitting there chewing on jerky, drinking real coffee, and eating freshly baked bread, I wondered if there could be a man anywhere in the world as happy and content as I was just then. I doubted that there was.

Figuring that I wouldn't want to be spooking the game where I put my canoe up for the night, I decided to shoot myself something for supper on the island before I left.

Taking up my rifle, I took off at a slow trot into the surrounding woods. My luck was still holding, for within five minutes a grouse stopped broadside to me about thirty yards away. Now, if I hadn't had a full belly, I would have aimed for the body. But being that I had just eaten and knowing that the best meat on a grouse is on the breast, I tried for a head shot. When the smoke cleared, I saw that my gamble had payed off. The lead ball had severed the bird's head as neatly as any butcher's axe.

Dressing the grouse, I placed it in the shaded bottom part of the boat where I knew that it would remain cool until supper.

As I floated down the river, eyeballing the scenery along its banks, I was beginning to wonder if at twenty-five cents a day I wasn't being overpaid. But then I remembered that I wasn't being paid to float down the river but to provide meat for forty people. And so far I hadn't even earned the bread and coffee I had for lunch.

It was a good hour before dark, but I had spotted the perfect place for a camp on the Kentucky side of the river. So I pulled in and set up camp. That night, after setting out trotlines baited with jerky along the banks of the river, I sat down to a fine supper of roasted grouse, beans, coffee, and what some people called snake bread because of the way it swirled around the green stick it was cooked on.

The night was peaceful but my mind wasn't. Tomorrow I would start earning my keep. It was a big job feeding forty people. And I wondered if there would be enough game in the area to do it. The country around the river was starting to fill up. And with hard times affecting everybody, more and more people would be after wild game to supplement their larders. And when too many people settle in one place they destroy the game. I was young but I had seen places hunted out. It reminded me of what happens to ground that is farmed too much. Pretty soon nothing would grow there anymore.

It was the same with animals. You hunt them too much or kill the females during the birthing season, you just naturally cut down the number of animals available. But the people who didn't live in or near the woods couldn't see this. For all they knew was that there had always been game and there always would be. I wondered if they would learn before it was too late. Well, I couldn't solve the problem by myself, so I lay there and allowed the sounds of the river to lull me to sleep.

Chapter Three
Matt Earns His Keep

The first streaks of light had just begun to appear as I rested my back against a giant oak I had climbed thirty minutes earlier. Sitting twenty feet above the ground, I had an excellent view of a vast expanse of flat ground between two hills with a creek running through it. There were several game trails leading to the stream, leading me to believe that the area was game-rich, and from my perch, I hoped to find plenty of targets.

To my way of thinking there's nothing like being in the deep woods early in the morning when everything is starting to stir to life. And from my vantage point I had a unique view of the wildlife. I was especially interested in a grove of hickory trees about fifty yards in front of me. From the way the leaves were shaking with no wind blowing, I knew that those trees had to be full of squirrels cuttin' on the hickory nuts on the limbs. And while squirrels smothered in red-eye gravy were to be savored, I needed bigger game if I was going to feed forty people. Then, as if in answer to my unspoken prayer, a fat, seven-point buck ghosted into view, headed for the creek.

28

Easing the rifle to my shoulder, I sighted down the long barrel of the muzzle-loader, putting its front sight behind his left shoulder and firing off a shot.

Straining to see around the black powder smoke, I saw the deer run about fifty feet from where he had been shot, try to force his way through some thick brush, and then fall.

On the hunt I always carried my powder in pre-measured charges inside a corked reed. Unstopping one of those reeds, I poured the powder down the muzzle, removed a pre-cut patch from the patch box in the stock, placed it over the barrel with a lead ball on top, and rammed the whole affair home with the ramrod. I finished the job by placing a percussion cap on the nipple. I didn't bother bringing the hammer down to half-cock since I knew that it wouldn't be long before I fired the rifle again.

Within five minutes another buck moved silently beneath my tree. A spine shot dropped the animal instantly. Climbing down from the tree, I moved slowly toward the squirrels, reloading the rifle as I went. Within an hour I had shot fifteen squirrels. Many of them had been taken two at a time with one ball. And once I had managed a triple. And I was always careful of the meat. I always took head shots or shot the bark under them to avoid too much damage. For squirrels didn't have that much meat on them to begin with. But fried up with red-eye gravy and biscuits they would make a nice change from all the venison. And while I wouldn't be doing any of the cooking, I planned to give the ones who would be doing it as much of a choice as I could.

I was relaxing on the river bank when I noticed the flat-boats coming into view. The deer were dressed out and hanging from trees in the woods. The squirrels were skinned and cut up ready for the cook pot. On a stringer in the water lay four catfish, with not one weighing less than thirty pounds. On the bank lay a fifty-pound snapping turtle, also caught on the trot line.

Rink's crew knew their business. It was obvious that he had his men on each boat, for they docked with a clocklike precision. After checking to see that everything was all squared away on the boats, he wandered up the bank to check on my work.

It was quite a sight the way that Rink and his men set up a camp. They didn't seem to waste any motion. The deer were quickly skinned and quartered. The settlers started cook fires as Rink's men distributed the meat. I could see that these were tough people who would do well no matter what the situation. Watching them work was a pure pleasure.

Carrying a rifle scabbard and another sack, Rink made his way back up the bank to me.

Smiling, he said, "Mr. Coltrane, you sure earned your salt today. Matter of fact, I think we need to talk about the terms of your employment."

I was more than a little nervous when I heard that. I sort of had a vision of Ezra Jensen for a minute there. And being that I was happy with the arrangement I had, I didn't want to fix something that wasn't broke.

"When you first hired on back at Maysville I didn't know what kind of job you could do, so I held back on my offer." Opening the flap on the scabbard, he withdrew a shiny new rifle with a highly polished walnut stock. It was the most beautiful gun I had ever seen in my life.

"It's a Winchester '73. Oliver Winchester's newest model. It's a lever action 44-40. It's accurate and dependable," he said, handing me the rifle. "Stick with me to New Orleans and the gun's yours. Get killed along the way and I send it to your nearest relative along with your wages."

I just sat there rubbing my hand over that well-oiled walnut stock and not believing my own good luck.

"You will probably need the firepower that rifle will give you. Not necessarily for the game you hunt. There are still bandits on this river and more than a few settlers around who ain't quite honest and would have no problem shooting you for whatever you had in that canoe. Or for that matter, the canoe itself. Some people along the river would kill you for the clothes you're wearing."

I heard what he was saying about the danger and all, but I just stared down at that rifle. There were people back home who would have done just about anything for a gun like that. Including me.

Remembering my manners, I stammered out a "Thank you."

"Don't worry, son, before this trip is over you will have earned it," he said. Digging into the sack and bringing out two boxes of .44 cartridges, he tossed them to me. "You'll be needin' those."

After checking the barrel to see that there was no gun grease in it, I broke open one of the cartridge boxes and started stuffing shells through the rifle's loading gate.

Digging back in the sack, he came out with a shell belt and a holster. Inside the holster was a revolver held in place by a leather thong looped over the hammer. Slipping the loop off the hammer, he took out the gun and examined it.

Handing it to me he said, "You'll be needing this too."

Taking the weapon, I marveled at how smooth the walnut grips were and how it just seemed so well balanced and natural in my hand.

"It's a Colt. Same caliber as the rifle. I prefer a .45 myself but given your situation, I think having both guns using the same ammunition should simplify things quite a bit for you."

Allowing me to get the feel of the handgun for a few minutes, he continued, "The barrel is five and a half inches long. Two inches shorter than mine. But I believe it will allow you to draw quicker and it won't be in your way as much in cramped quarters like the canoe as the longer barrel would have been."

Standing, he handed me the belt. It had several shell loops in it.

"I've found that if you are right-handed that when you are standing or walking it is best to wear the handgun on your right side with the gun butt pointing to the rear. On horseback or in a canoe, I prefer to wear it on my left side, gun butt forward."

Bowing to his experience, I strapped the Colt on my right side as we walked to the river bank. Picking up a piece of driftwood, Rink flung it into the river.

"See if you can hit that before the current takes it out of range."

He didn't have to tell me twice, for I was fairly bustin' to try out that gun. The rifle butt came to my shoulder all natural-like. The lever action was as smooth as butter as I worked the lever, jacking a shell into the chamber. I squeezed the trigger and that piece of wood sailed in an arc across the river. Two more shots and that piece of driftwood was nothing but a memory.

"Well, son, you don't need no practice with a rifle. What about the short gun? You used one much?"

Stuffing shells back into the Winchester to bring it up to its capacity of fifteen rounds, I answered, "No sir."

Taking another chunk of driftwood he threw it into a pool of water on the bank of the river. Pointing at it, he said, "Try it."

Now, I had fired a muzzle-loading pistol a time or two but I wasn't no great shakes with one. But it seems my reflexes took over. The Colt came out of the holster, leveled, and fired, with the driftwood jumping out of the pool and landing near the river. Thumbing the hammer back, I fired again, knocking the chunk of wood into the river. The current caught it, forcing me to hurry my remaining shots. One shot hit the target and the other two missed. The two shots were close to the target and if it had been a man I had shot at, he would have been dead.

Reloading, I dropped the Colt back in its holster. "Need to work on my handgun skills."

"You're already better with that hogleg than most men I've seen who make their living with one. That's an important skill out West. But be careful about getting a reputation. There's plenty of young toughs out there who want that kind of a reputation and if they found out you were that good, you'd never have a moment's peace. There'd always be some fool at your door wanting to get shot."

Sniffing the air, Rink commented, "Smells like supper will be ready soon. Best be getting back."

Walking back, Rink noticed the thong was off the Colt's hammer. "Best to keep the thong on the hammer when you're on the river since you might tip the canoe and lose it." And then he remembered another crucial point. "It's also important to remember to always leave the hammer down on an empty chamber. Less likely to blow your own foot off that way."

"Yes sir," I said, acknowledging the advice.

We ate supper that night by several campfires. And there was quite a feast that night. Someone had taken the squirrels I'd shot, seasoned them, and put them in a pot with bread dough and made some mouthwatering squirrel and dumplings. It was a big hit with everybody. Myself, now, I was so used to eating game and getting my supper from the woods that I was just plumb taken with soup beans and cornbread. And there was plenty of both that night so I had my fill.

Later that night I slept the sleep of the just with my new weapons very close at hand.

Morning came early and I was ready to shove off two hours before dawn. That was because I needed those two hours to do my hunting and have the game ready for all those hungry folks when they pulled into shore.

I'd been floating along for three hours before I found a likely spot for game. Rowing the canoe into shore, I quickly set out my trotlines and melted into the woods. The new rifle proved to be quite a provider. Within four hours I had a deer, two turkeys, three rabbits, and a grouse. Or as the people back home called it, a mountain pheasant. It was a rare treat to sit down at the supper table to enjoy one of those fast-flying birds. They were hard targets even with a shotgun, which made the way I had downed that particular bird even more remarkable.

I'd been dressing out the deer when I heard the leaves rustle to my left. My rifle had been leaning against a tree twenty feet away. Dropping the knife, I spun to my left and drew the pistol. I suppose being scared pushed me to draw fast, for the speed with which I brought that Colt out of the holster surprised even me. The grouse spooked and took flight. The 44-40 bucked in my hand and the fat bird just folded in mid-air and dropped to the ground. I was certainly getting better with that pistol gun.

Returning to where I had docked the canoe, I laid the game in the canoe and took up the trotlines which had two heavy catfish on their hooks. Lashing them to the side of the canoe, I shoved off from the bank, grabbed the paddle, and put my back into digging the oar into the water. I was sure that Rink was ahead of me and I would have to make time if I hoped to catch him before dark. If I didn't get there in time I'd be met by a bunch of hungry people with hard looks on their faces.

It would be dark in a few hours and I figured to catch the boats just about dusk. With that goal in mind, I dug the oar deep into the river, pushing the boat on. I was so intent in my effort to catch the boats that I heard the voice before I saw the man.

"We got whiskey!" a voice from the bank announced.

I slipped the thong off the Colt's hammer and scanned the cliffs above the river. I saw a bearded man with a gut that hung over his belt holding a whiskey jug in the air and standing at the mouth of a cave.

"Got me a still back there," he said, pointing to the back of the cave. "Good corn liquor. Come on up and have a drink."

"No thanks," I replied, digging the paddle deep into the water. "Got somewhere I gotta be."

Water spouted violently in front of my boat, followed by the echo of a large caliber rifle. Looking up, I saw that old Big-gut had a buffalo gun aimed at my head. And now four other men were with him, each one loaded down with hardware, and everyone of them was pointing a pistol or rifle at me.

"Boy, you just ease that canoe over here and you won't get hurt none," old Big-gut said, motioning with his rifle.

Now, while I was young, I wasn't wet behind the ears. I knew from the looks of that bunch on the cliff they had no intention of leaving any witnesses to point them out to a judge. So I pulled that Colt in cross-draw fashion with my right hand and started firing as fast as I could thumb the hammer back.

Big-gut toppled forward over the cliff. The others scrambled for cover. From the screams I heard I figured my bullets had bounced around quite a bit inside that cave. But I knew I hadn't killed them all because of all of the cussin' I heard.

Holstering the empty Colt, I took up the Winchester and jacked a shell into its chamber. Covering the mouth of the cave with the long gun, I let the current carry me to safety. Only one of that bunch had the nerve to stick his head out of that cave and I rewarded him with another hole in the battered old hat that he wore. I'd meant to shoot over his head, but I had misjudged the distance and the bullet fell a mite lower than I intended. Anyway, the hat went sailing off his head toward the back of the cave with him following close behind it. The rest of his friends lacked his curiosity so I floated on out of range with no more gun play.

An hour later I paddled on into camp, where Rink's men swarmed over the game in my canoe like locusts attacking a wheat field.

Motioning for me to join him, Rink said, "Light and set a spell, Matt. We got coffee on."

Cradling the rifle in my arm, I squatted by the fire and took the coffee offered by one of the settler's wives.

"Heard what sounded like a war going on upriver a little while back. Did you see what happened?" he asked.

"I saw it," I answered. "Matter of fact, I guess you could say I had a front-row seat for the whole thing."

Rink stiffened. "What happened?"

"Five men in a cave a few miles back thought they would make themselves richer by relieving me of my goods. We discussed the matter a mite and they decided that they didn't want my stuff after all. I'm surprised they didn't offer to help you out the same way."

Rink chuckled. "Have you taken a good look at my crew and passsengers, Matt?"

I have to admit that I really hadn't paid all that much attention to them, so I looked them over and saw what Rink was talking about. Every one of Rink's crew members packed a repeating rifle and a revolver. The settlers were also well-heeled, carrying everything from muzzle-loading shotguns to the newest rifles.

Now it was my turn to laugh. "I see what you mean. They would have to have been plumb loco to have tackled this bunch." I downed the last of my coffee.

Rink smiled and said, "Given the fact that you just shot it out with them and didn't get a scratch, it appears that it ain't too wise to tackle you either."

"I got lucky."

"I've seen you shoot, Matt. It ain't luck." He rose to his feet and walked over to give one of his men some orders.

Walking over to the fire, I refilled my cup. "I hope you're right," I said, staring out over the river. "I sure hope you're right."

Chapter Four
Marie Laborteaux

The following days were fairly tame. Oh, there had been a few people who had made an attempt to rob me. But a few well-placed rounds from my Winchester changed their minds. Of course, no one offered to bother Rink and his boats.

It wasn't until I was about to pass by the Arkansas border that something occurred that was to forever change my life.

Rounding a turn in the river, I ended up pretty much in the center of the waterway where I spotted something on the west bank that was very much out of place. On a mat of dry, dead leaves there was a flash of color not seen in nature. Taking a closer look I could see that it was a woman in a dress who was tied and gagged.

While I had run across similar situations before, there was something different about this one. People had called out from the bank before claiming injuries, offering food or whiskey in an attempt to get me to the shore where they could rob me. But Rink had warned me about such tactics and I had gotten pretty good at being able to spot a setup. And while I was sure that what I was looking at was a setup, everything in my gut told me that the woman on shore was in genuine trouble. But I had no intention of charging over to that riverbank.

Slipping the thong off the Colt's hammer, I dug the paddle deep into the water, speeding on down the river, all the while keeping an eye peeled toward that west bank.

After traveling a mile, I pulled into the bank on the Arkansas side of the river and jumped ashore, taking to the woods and heading upriver at a lope.

Circling the area where I figured the girl to be, I soon found three drunken men passing around a whiskey bottle. The woman, or more accurately, the girl, was tied to a tree, and from where I stood she didn't appear to be much older than sixteen.

Crouching at the edge of their camp, I listened to the one I assumed to be the leader bad-mouthing me. He was a short skinny man with ears so big that they had to be a danger to him in high winds.

"Never did see so gutless a man as that feller in the canoe. What kind of a man leaves a helpless woman all alone on a riverbank?"

Stepping into their camp, I said, "A careful one." The Colt was in my hand and I had eared back the hammer.

I doubted that those gents were much when it came to thinking when they were sober, and since they'd been drinking pretty heavy, I was wary about how they would react.

My sudden appearance had just about caused them to jump out of their skins. But once they saw I was just one man, they came at me with everything they had. One pulled a knife, another was swinging a club, and Big-ears was trying to pull an old Dragoon pistol from inside the waistband of his pants.

I was in something of a quandary. I had to stop these

fools before they did me some major damage, but I wasn't inclined to shoot a bunch of drunks. So I did the only thing I could think of doing at the time. Instead of shooting to kill, I shot to disable. Picking the one closest to me which happened to be the man with the club, I drilled him in the foot. He promptly fell, tripping the one with the knife. Swinging back to Big-ears, I was just in time to witness him extract the pistol from his pants and deftly shoot off his own toe.

Walking over to where he dropped the pistol, I scooped it up and moved over to the man with the knife who was just getting to his feet, and laid the heavy barrel of the weapon alongside his head.

Deciding it would be a wise policy to disarm such careless people as they were proving to be, I relieved them of all of their weapons and tossed them in the river.

Giving them a quick once-over, I decided that they were no longer a threat.

Slipping my knife from its scabbard, I cut the rawhide bindings holding the girl to the tree.

"Can you walk?" I asked, removing the gag from her mouth.

She nodded and quickly stood. Thinking I would have to slow my pace, I was surprised that she could easily match my stride and so within a few minutes we covered the mile back and had launched the canoe.

She said very little as we moved down the river. I explained about the people I worked for and she only nodded, letting me know that she had heard what I had said. I was pretty curious about her but I could see that she didn't want to talk about what had happened to her. And I could see that she kept watching the riverbank to see if anyone was following us. I also noticed that she was a very pretty girl.

Her hair was coal black and I figured that normally her

skin would have been a soft milky white—the type city girls prized so highly. But the sun had turned hers to a tan color. And from the callouses on her small hand I had no doubt that she had spent a lot of time in the fields helping her family put up crops. There was definitely steel in her for she had every right to fall apart after what had happened to her. Instead, she fell into line and did what was necessary. I admired that kind of grit in anybody. It seemed especially nice when it was found in someone so young and pretty.

I was used to people eyeballing me when I came into shore; after all, I was packing their supper. But this evening I had their complete attention. Or I should say *she* had their complete attention. And it wasn't just because she was a stranger. It seemed that my opinion of her beauty was shared by the crew and passengers of our little expedition.

Seeing her back stiffen, I said, "Don't worry, they're good people. They're just curious. It's not every day they see a pretty young girl floating down the river in a canoe." Glancing back at me, she nodded.

As soon as the boat touched shore she jumped out and tied it to a tree stump. Rink was beside her in a second. "What happened, Matt?"

Picking up my rifle, I stepped onto the bank. "Bandits were using her as bait to lure travelers to shore so they could rob them. I got her away from the pirates."

"They put up much of a fuss?" asked Rink.

"Some," I answered.

Nodding, Rink turned toward the crowd. "Mrs. Warren!" he shouted.

A large matronly woman pushed her way through the crowd. Rink spoke with her for a few minutes, explaining the situation.

Taking the girl by the hand, Mrs. Warren said, "Come along, dear." And led her through the crowd.

Later that night I got to hear the whole story on the girl I had freed. Her name was Marie Laborteaux. She was seventeen years old and had just lost her whole family to the river pirates. I found out that her family had owned a farm near the river where they raised their crops and sold them to people who traveled the river. They had been doing this for as long as she could remember. She hadn't known any of the men who had attacked her pa's farm. She figured that they were people they had traded with before. Or they could have been folks who figured that they had laid up a big pile of money over the years from all the trading they had done on the river. It wasn't true, for nobody got rich farming in that part of the country.

Her father had seen them coming and had sent her to the woods. Hearing the shots as she ran, she knew her family was doomed. Still she stayed hidden for a full day like her father had told her. Finally, tired of waiting, she returned to the farm and found that everything had been torn down and burned. Nothing had been left standing.

She managed to hold her emotions in check long enough to bury her parents and younger brother. And then she broke down, sobbing at their graves. In her grief, she failed to see the three pirates sneaking up on her and was therefore captured by them.

From listening to them talk during the night she discovered that they had been with the party that had destroyed the farm. Unfortunately for them, they had performed so poorly during the raid that the other bandits kicked them out of the group. And being left alone to make their own way, they returned to the farm in hopes of finding something the rest of the group had missed. That had been what they were doing when they captured her at the graves. They considered it quite a stroke of good luck to capture her, for now they could use her as bait to pull in dumb pilgrims traveling on the river. I was supposed to be the first victim.

Sipping my coffee, I chuckled to myself when I thought of how incompetent one would have to be for a band of thieves to throw you out. And to have your first attempt at piracy end up with one man knocked cold and the other two with a gunshot wound to the foot. And worst of all, one of the wounds was self-inflicted.

I was stirred from my reverie by a soft voice. "I would like to thank you, Mr. Coltrane, for saving me from those men."

I stood so quickly that I smacked my head on a low-hanging limb of the tree I had been sitting under. "Excuse me, ma'am, I didn't see you come up," I stammered.

"Oh my!" she said, motioning for me to return to my seat. "Please sit back down."

I don't know what it is about a pretty girl asking a man to do something that makes him jump to do it. Even if he didn't want to do it. And everything in my upbringing had taught me to stand when a lady spoke to me. But there I was, sitting back down like a well-trained dog. And then, seeming to sense my discomfort, she joined me on the ground.

Seeing that she was wearing a new dress, I asked, "How are things going with the Warrens?"

"Oh, they're wonderful people," she said, touching the collar of the dress. "They gave me this. It belonged to one of their daughters. They are very generous people."

Ordinarily I would't have been so nosy about someone else's business, but I had saved her life and felt like I had sort of a responsibility to her. Or maybe I was just taken with getting a chance to talk to a pretty girl. Especially one who probably thought of me as some sort of a hero.

"What are your plans?" I asked. A terrible look of sadness came over her face and I immediately felt sorry for having asked the question.

"The Warrens have asked me to go with them to New Orleans. They need help with some of their younger children, and they said that another pair of willing hands was always welcome on a farm."

Sighing, she looked off toward the far bank. "I'll go with them, because there wasn't anything left on our farm in Arkansas after the pirates left. Everything was burned to the ground."

I never was worth shucks when it came to talking to females. I had a bad habit of saying exactly what I was thinking. And I believed in diving right in and getting to the point. Womenfolk seemed to prefer men who could be subtle and dance all around a subject without once getting to the point.

"I'm glad," I said.

Seeing her turn to look at me, it dawned on me what I had said must have sounded like. "No! I didn't mean it the way it sounded. I'm not glad that your farm burned down. What I meant was that I was glad you're coming to New Orleans with us," I said, my face turning red from embarrassment.

She laughed. "Oh, I knew that," she said, touching my hand.

I could really feel the color creeping up my neck now. The last time I had experienced a feeling like I was having now, I had been standing too near a tree that was being struck by lightning.

I smiled at her, not trusting myself to say the right thing. I've always found that when you've already stuck one foot in your mouth it's best to get that one out before sticking the other foot in the same place.

Taking the lead in helping me save face, she said, "I understand that you've been supplying the meat for all these people."

"All the way from Maysville, Kentucky, on the Ohio River," I answered.

"That's a pretty big responsibility for someone so young," she said.

"I've been lucky."

"Not according to Mr. Rink. He says that you're his best man. And it's not just him singing your praises. Several people have told me how lucky I was that it was you who found me. They said you were the best with a gun they had ever seen."

Well, if the color that once again was creeping up my neck was going to keep doing that, I was going to have to run off and hide to keep from dying of embarrassment.

But once again seeing that I was getting uncomfortable, she came to my rescue. Pointing at my Winchester, she said, "That's a nice rifle. I had an old muzzle-loader I used to use around the farm. Pa was too busy to hunt, so that job fell to me and I grew to love the times I spent in the woods along the river. And my pa really enjoyed the game I brought home for the supper table. I wish that those men could have left that old gun. Reaching over to some rolled up blankets I pulled my old squirrel rifle out. "I've been packing this in the canoe for a lot of miles. Not that I really need it but because I didn't really have anyone to leave it with. If it would comfort you any you'd be doing me a favor by holding on to it for me until we get to New Orleans. You never know when you might find it useful."

Taking the rifle she said, "I'd be pleased to pack this squirrel gun, Mr. Coltrane."

Handing her the sack containing the powder and shot, I said, "I suppose that since you'll be doing me a favor by carrying that old piece of iron, you really should start calling me Matt."

Taking the sack, she said, "Then you will just have to call me Marie."

The rest of the trip proved uneventful. The only interesting part of it now was learning about Marie. She told me that she had a French father and an Irish mother. She claimed she got her looks from her father and her temper from her mother. Although I couldn't say that her temper was that bad. I considered it to be downright sweet. But then again, I didn't have all that much to compare it to. Since my mother's passing I'd mostly been among men. And none of them had been known for their manners or refinement. I suppose I considered anybody who didn't cuss on Sunday or spit into your fireplace when supper was on to be well mannered.

I also discovered during some of those long talks we had around the campfire at night that she had relatives in Louisiana. And some of them were living in New Orleans. When I asked if she planned to look them up, she told me that they were from her father's side of the family and he had always told her never to associate with them. She didn't know why her father never associated with them, but Marie had gotten the impression that they were dangerous people and it was smart to leave them alone at all costs. He had warned her that if she ever met someone who resembled her or her father to head for different country and not leave a trail. She had asked him why, but he had only said that it was a matter of life or death and to mind what he told her.

Ordinarily I would have been itching with curiosity about a story like she told me about her father's family, but it seemed that just about every person I met on the river had something mysterious about them. And when it was stacked up against some of the stories about some of the other people traveling the river with me, it didn't seem all that unusual.

Chapter Five
New Orleans

I had paddled on to New Orleans ahead of Rink's flatboats and was waiting on shore when the others arrived. I started to mosey on over to Rink when two citified gents pushed by, almost knocking me into the water. Recovering my balance, I could see one of them stick his hand out to Rink and ask, "Everything go all right, Rink?"

"Everything is fine, Mr. Argyle," Rink said to the short fat man who had extended his hand.

"I've rented rooms for your passengers, Rink, and I've brought wagons to transport them to the hotel where the rooms are. I've also made arrangements to stable their animals."

"Good," said Rink, as he turned to face the people disembarking from the boats. Motioning toward the wagons, he spoke to the people. "There's your transportation, folks. Load your goods and yourselves onto those wagons and you will be taken to where you will be boarded."

The people began carrying their valuables over to the wagons and loading them aboard. I walked over to the Warrens with the stated intention of helping them load, but with

48

the actual intention of having a few words with Marie. But I was brought up short by Rink's voice. "Mr. Coltrane, a word with you if you please."

Walking over to where he and Argyle stood, I looked at him questioningly.

"Mr. Argyle, young Coltrane here is my best man. I believe that any man in my crew will tell you that he's a man to ride the river with. If it hadn't been for his skills we would have gone hungry many a night, not to mention the time we would have lost if we had to stop to hunt meat for ourselves. But this young man went out every day on his own, risking his life so that the rest of us could enjoy a fine supper around the campfire at night."

Mr. Argyle shook my hand. "Such praise from a man like John Rink really means something, young man. As a matter of fact," he said, turning to Rink, "you have all done such outstanding jobs that I think bonuses are called for all the way around. And just as soon as the shipment is delivered to the bank, I'll pay that along with your regular salaries."

I didn't know what shipment he meant but I did know what a bonus was and that it seemed I was to get one. And then Argyle seemed to become nervous and agitated. Walking up the bank a way he checked to make sure that the wagons carrying the passengers were out of sight and that there wasn't anybody around who wasn't there normally. When he appeared to be satisfied that there wasn't anything out of the ordinary, he motioned to a man standing in front of a building who quickly walked behind the structure.

I was beginning to wonder if everybody who lived in big towns like New Orleans acted so peculiar, when I saw the man who had been standing in front of the building come out from behind it driving a large freight wagon being pulled by four horses. I recognized the man driving the rig as the man who had walked up to Rink earlier. I also noticed that Rink's crew was acting mighty uncomfortable for some reason as the freight wagon pulled up to the flatboats. They were dividing their attention between the freight wagon and watching Rink for some kind of a signal. I found myself doing the same thing and happened to have my attention on Rink when I noticed him give a slight nod toward the men on the boats. At once they began to break out pry bars and started prying and ripping planks off the sides of the flatboats. Soon they were carrying leather sacks that appeared to be extremely heavy and loading them on the wagon.

Now I may have been just a country boy and young to boot, but I knew that what was in those sacks had to be gold. Rink saw me looking and catching my eye, he smiled. Right about then I felt like three different kinds of a fool. I hadn't had a clue about what had actually been going on during the last two months. I wondered about how much gold I had been sleeping next to all those nights.

Sensing my unasked question as he walked up beside me, Rink said, "A little over a million dollars."

I could only whistle at the very thought of all that gold out in the wilderness and what would have happened to us if word of our secret cargo had got out. I remembered what Rink had said about how certain people who lived along the river would have killed me for the clothes I wore.

"From the look on your face, I can tell that you are thinking about what people would have done to get their hands on all that gold," said Rink. "I hope you're not offended by my not telling you about the cargo."

"Given the same set of circumstances, I would have done the same thing," I answered honestly.

Slapping me on the back, he said, "Good! Only the five men in my crew knew what I was hauling, and they were all hand-picked men. Still, I only told them because I had to have their help in guarding the shipment. When it comes to gold it is best not to trust anyone. For there is something about that yellow metal that can change a man's soul, with the most honest and steady men in the world sometimes going loco from just the sight of it."

Watching his men load the last of the cargo, Rink took a cigar from his pocket. "Matt, when we settle our accounts at the bank I would like to talk to you about working for me on a full-time basis. You see, I have something of a reputation as the kind of a man you look up when something valuable has to be transported under dangerous circumstances. And I can always use somebody like you."

Feeling the weight of the Winchester in the crook of my arm and the Colt strapped to my waist, I said, "Be happy to talk to you about it," I said. And I sure meant it. Since having signed on with Mr. Rink, I had half of the outfit I needed to get a job riding herd and I hadn't had to use my own money to buy anything for the last two months. Plus there was the fact that I was going to be paid a salary plus a bonus. And best of all, I was in a state that bordered Texas. I didn't see how things could get any better.

One of the crew shouted that they were ready. Rink, turning to face me, said, "You've been drawing warrior's wages since you signed up back on the Ohio. And the last job I have for you is to ride shotgun with me on this cargo till we get to the bank."

"All right," I said, hopping into the wagon and settling down among all those leather bags of gold. Argyle joined the man driving the wagon on the front seat with the rest of Rink's crew following on horses that had been supplied by Argyle. Rink took up a position at the front of the wagon while I stayed at the rear.

No one tried anything on the way to the bank. I suppose

it was much the same as it had been on the boats. It would have taken somebody who was either very desperate or crazy to jump a bunch of men who fairly bristled with firearms. The buildings on the street surrounding the bank spoke of a great deal of wealth. And from the looks of the vault I helped carry that gold into, I had no doubt that once something went behind that locked door, it stayed there until Argyle released it.

After all of the gold was safely locked in the vault, Argyle set up his books at his desk and began paying the men off. I waited outside with the rest of the men as Rink called everyone in one at a time. I figured that since I was the last one hired, and being the youngest, I would be paid last. I said good-bye to each man as he took his pay and headed for town. While I was cordial with all of them, I hadn't really made any friendships with any of them because of the nature of my job. Hunting meat all day kept me away from camp most of the time.

My assumption that I would be the last called in proved to be right. The last of Rink's regular crew, a man named Brooks, hooked his thumb in the direction of the door and told me that I was next and then hurried off toward somewhere he could find some relief for the money burning a hole in his pocket.

Walking through the door I noticed Argyle motioning for me to sit in a chair in front of his desk. Rink was standing beside the desk keeping his own tally book.

I suppose I looked pretty smug sitting there. According to my figures, I was owed fifteen whole dollars and a bonus. I figured the bonus to be as much as two dollars.

Looking through his tally book, Rink said, "Mr. Coltrane, when I hired you on back in Maysville I told you that I was paying you at the rate of two bits a day. In truth, I put you on the books as a gun hand. A gun hand makes a bit more than two bits a day. It comes to one hundred dollars."

After hearing the amount announced, Argyle began counting out one hundred dollars in gold coins in front of me.

Well, all I could say was that I was glad that I was sitting down because that wasn't the only shock I was in for that day. I had no sooner scooped up the coins and put them into my possibles bag than Argyle began to count out ten more silver dollars.

"This is the bonus I spoke of earlier," he said, shoving the silver across the desk.

Anyone who saw me about then would have thought I was trying to catch flies with my mouth open the way it was. Stunned, I managed to stammer out a thanks to both of them and head for the door.

Rink reminded me that he wanted to have a few words with me and asked if I would mind waiting for him a few minutes.

"Sure,"I said and walked outside to wait for him. I didn't have to wait long, for he soon finished his business with Argyle and joined me on the streets of New Orleans.

"Have you given any thought about coming to work for me full-time, Matt?" he asked.

"I haven't decided just yet but I sure plan on giving it some serious thought," I said.

"Good," he replied. "And just a word to the wise, Matt. You're packing a lot of money and the woods ain't half as dangerous as a big town can be. There's plenty of people here who can show you a dozen different ways to separate you from your money."

Walking along with him I said, "I figured as much. I guess I'll get cleaned up, buy a suit of clothes, and see the town."

"Might you be planin' on a visit to a certain dark-haired girl?" Rink asked, a grin on his face.

I could feel the blood rushing up my neck again, causing it to color. I suppose only a fool wouldn't have noticed my growing interest in Marie Laborteux. Especially since I kept finding important reasons to speak to her. And obviously it hadn't gone unnoticed. I was embarrassed but I saw no reason to deny that I was attracted to her.

"Yep, I've grown right fond of her, I guess."

Rink chuckled. "I reckon I should have warned you about how dangerous the female race can be. They can be especially crafty when it comes to snaring unsuspecting, fumble-footed country boys."

We walked on to a store that had several suits on display. There we parted company after he gave me the name of the hotel where all of his crew was staying.

I'd never owned a store-bought suit before, but now that I had some money I thought it might be a good time to buy one. I also needed some new everyday-type outfits or folks were going to start calling me Patches instead of Matt. And for good reason. My pants were nothing but patches and even my buckskin shirt was pretty much worn out. And it wasn't just that they were worn out but that they were also too small. During the last two months on the river, with all the good food I had been shoveling down my throat along with the exercise I was getting from paddling that canoe, I had put on about ten pounds and developed my muscles and shoulders until every stitch of clothes that I owned was stretched almost to the breaking point.

After dickering with the owner of the shop for several minutes, I was the proud owner of three new pairs of jeans and three shirts, along with socks and underwear. The owner was also a tailor so the deal included one of his new suits, altered to fit my new frame. He said it would be ready in two days. Possibly one day, with a little luck.

Putting on my newly bought Stetson hat, I walked out of that store leaving behind my old clothes and fifteen silver dollars.

Expecting the hotel where our rooms had been rented for us to be on the cheap side, I was pleasantly surprised to see that it was a first-class establishment. I was beginning to understand that Rink didn't do anything on the cheap. His outfit was first-class all the way.

A bath and a shave and I was ready to find a place to eat. Inquiring at the desk, I was informed by a rather snooty clerk that when one was in New Orleans one didn't ask about which establishment was best. All of the restaurants in the town were outstanding. All you had to do was ask where the nearest eatery was located. And in that case, it was a place known as the Red Boar, three blocks north of the hotel.

Walking in the door, I spotted a couple of Rink's crew. No doubt I hadn't been steered wrong about how good the food would be. I took a table in the back of the room where I could see who came in the tavern and keep an eye on those who were already there. I figured it to be a good idea to exercise caution, for Rink had told me to always be careful around establishments where I didn't see any ladies because the place could turn rowdy in a hurry. And although I had stopped by Argyle's bank to deposit most of my money, I was still packing a sizable amount of cash and I didn't want to risk it in some stupid bar fight or lose it to some light-fingered pickpocket.

Settling in, I ordered the biggest steak they had and asked them to smother it with taters. After finishing that off, I downed two big chunks of apple pie along with three cups of what they called French coffee.

It was a great meal. I guess that snooty clerk was right. Anyway, I intended to find out for myself by visiting a few more of these eateries before I left this town. At least that was what I was thinking when I leaned back in my chair and loosened my belt. But then the waiter come over with what they called a check which was just a fancy name for a bill. Well, I suppose if you are going to charge a man one dollar and two bits for some grub, you might as well put a fancy name to it. I was inclined to call it robbery. Standing, I counted out the money and laid it on the check. And then remembering that Rink had told me it was customary to leave what was known as a tip for the waiter, I fished out a nickel and put it by the coffee cup.

Standing outside, I was beginning to wonder if some of the pickpockets and thieves in this town had started to open up restaurants. After all, overcharging for a meal was a whole lot safer than robbing somebody outright. And you never got a tip for picking someone's pocket. I suppose you couldn't tip a thief. What would you tip him with, since he had all your money?

After thinking about that for a few seconds I decided that the best thing to do was to get a bit of exercise and walk off that expensive meal. Picking a direction, I started putting one foot in front of the other. Walking fast, I covered a lot of ground until I began to lose the stuffed feeling I had from the steak and taters.

Deciding to head back to the hotel, I crossed the street so as to see what was in the different shops on the way back.

I was glancing at some kind of a gadget on display in a shop window when I was bumped into by a gent who appeared to have a weakness for corn whiskey. He fairly reeked of it and was trying to keep himself upright by grabbing for handholds on me.

"Sorry mis . . . mister," he said as he finally stood up straight, tipped his hat, and staggered on down the street.

While I was much better at figuring out what a four-legged critter was up to by the way it acted, I could tell there was something odd about the way that man was behaving. There was something about his gait that didn't ring true. It could have been my imagination, but it seemed that this man was staggering less with each step that he took.

Reaching into my pocket, I found that the leather poke I had been carrying coins in was missing. Putting two and two together, I took off after the pickpocket.

Glancing back when he heard me running, he amazed me at how fast he sobered up. And for a heavyset gent he could run like a deer and the way he could dodge in and out of alleyways would have done a rabbit proud. But I had grown up running through briar patches and up hills so steep that a man not running up them would have had to hold on to something just to stand on them. So it wasn't long before I caught up to him.

Grabbing him by the collar, I yanked him backward. He was winded but still had some fight left in him. Turning, he sank his teeth deep into my arm. Being unable to free my arm from his bulldog-like grip, I grabbed the lapel of his coat with my free hand and threw him into the brick wall of the building we were near. Releasing his grip on my arm, he fell to the ground on his butt.

Looking up at me, he started to put his hands under him to get back up. Facing him, I pulled the Colt and stuck it in his face and pulled back the hammer. "You stole my poke, forced me to chase you over half of creation, and bit me for my trouble. Now hand me my poke or get ready to eat some lead."

I suppose that old boy had been in a few fights and

maybe been cut a time or two, but he wanted no truck with my .44. He quietly handed over the leather pouch.

Stepping away from him, I dropped my weapon back in its holster. "If you ever see me on the street again, make sure I don't see you." Turning, I walked back up the street.

Continuing on my way to the hotel, I noticed a gunshop. And partly out of curiosity and partly out of need I went in. I had noticed that very few people wore their weapons out in the open around town, and my holstered rig was drawing more than a few stares. I needed a gun, but I wanted something a bit less noticeable.

The gunsmith looked like he had been around long enough to know his business. I had no doubt he could equip me with what I needed. "I think I have the very thing you're looking for," he said, taking a wooden case from behind his counter. Opening the box, he said, "This is a matched set of Remington .41 caliber derringers. They're nickel-plated and outfitted with genuine ivory grips." Hefting one and then the other, I checked the lockwork on each of them. It was obvious that the man who had assembled those pieces was a skilled craftsman. I had no doubt that they would shoot straight. Not that the range such a weapon would be used at would require pinpoint accuracy.

"How much with two boxes of shells?"

"Ten dollars, and a bargain at twice the price."

Looking them over once again, I said, "Don't know about that, mister. Back home a whole family could live on ten dollars for a winter. And I mean a big family during a hard winter."

The old man smiled. "I wouldn't know about that, son, but my price is still ten dollars."

I'd learned that arguing with these city folks over prices was a waste of time. Besides, one of the reasons that ten dollars could do mountain folks all winter was because when the the snow got bad the roads got blocked off and supplies couldn't make it in and there wasn't anything to buy. So I dug out ten dollars and laid them on the countertop.

"Despite what you think, son, you've made a good bargain. And I'll throw in some free advice." Taking one of the little guns from the case, he pulled the barrels down and loaded it with two shells and placed it in my shirt pocket.

"Lot of folks call it a vest gun. And that's where most people carry one. Other folks carry one in their boots. I've known men who have saved their lives by carrying them in both places."

Handing me the case, he said, "Remember, son, these aren't bear guns. They will only stop somebody if you hit them somewhere vital on their person. They're best used as a threat. Nobody wants to get shot no matter how small the gun. Remember that."

Taking up the case and boxes of ammunition, I said, "Thanks for the advice. I'd say it was sound wisdom."

Marie was looking out the window onto the street below when she saw me.

"Matt! Meet me downstairs in the lobby."

Bolting from the room, she ran for the stairs. Even I could hear Mrs. Warren laughing.

"Hello, Matt, I was wondering when I would see you again," she said, taking my hand and leading me over to the couch in the lobby. "I almost didn't recognize you in your new clothes."

"Been on the trail a long time, had a lot of things that needed doin'."

"I can see where you would," she said, touching the collar of my new shirt. "But for some reason I had grown right fond of those buckskins."

We spent the next hour telling each other about what had happened to each of us. From her I learned that the Warrens, along with some of the other settlers who had traveled down the river with us, were headed for Texas where they had bought some ranch land. They were all moving to a place called the Hill Country.

For my part, I told her about Rink's offer of employment and how I was considering it.

Finally the subject of the squirrel gun came up and I told her that no matter what I decided that I would still need to to store that old rifle somewhere and if she could still see her way clear to hold on to it for me, she would be doing me a big favor. She readily accepted.

"But I don't expect for you to store that old piece of iron for free," I said, opening the box containing the remaining derringer. "I would like for you to accept this as sort of a gift of appreciation for helping me out."

Taking the box, she said, "It's beautiful, and I don't just mean the gun but also the box."

I hadn't noticed before, but she was right. It was a beautiful rosewood case with brass fittings. It was just the type of thing that women liked to keep jewelry and little trinkets in.

Marie enjoyed getting her gift that evening and I enjoyed her company, but when I left her that evening other thoughts started to nag at me. I started remembering how things happened back in the hills of Kentucky. A boy and a girl would get married, both dreaming about their future together. But soon the children came along and they were both stuck on some hillside farm working from can see to can't see trying to make a living and feed a bunch of hungry mouths. Before they knew it they were old and used up wondering what had happened to their dreams.

I had escaped that fate once. I had been privilged to see how well life could be lived if a man could keep his freedom by staying single. But a marriage would be putting me in the same trap I had escaped in Kentucky. I also knew that I couldn't see Marie again. For if I did my resolve would melt faster than ice in July. My only chance to keep my freedom was to run. Leave Marie, forget about working for Rink, buy a horse and a saddle, and ride as fast as it could carry me. The only flaw in the plan was how I was going to tell Marie about what I was doing and why I was doing it, without seeing her again. Then it struck me—I could write a letter explaining everything, and have it delivered to her.

I spent a good part of that night writing that letter. The rest of the night I spent tossing in my bed.

I was up well before dawn the next morning. Not wanting to run into Marie or the Warrens or for that matter, I didn't feel like facing anyone I knew. I grabbed up all my gear and slinked out of the hotel.

I figured people in big towns stirred a lot later than country folks so I was surprised when I found a café open at such an early hour. But I wasn't really hungry so I just had coffee and whiled away the time until I figured the shops would start to open.

I bought a saddle, saddle bags, and a scabbard for my Winchester. Leaving them at the shop, I headed off to the stockyards to find a horse.

The man running the horse trading, seeing that I was young, took a run at trying to badger me into buying a wind-broke old nag. But I backed him off by saying, "My money—my choice." I decided on a chestnut stallion with long legs and that I figured to have plenty of bottom. The lowest price he would accept was fifty dollars in gold coin.

My fortune, obtained only one day ago, was rapidly shrinking. But I was as well outfitted as any Western man at the time.

I rode the horse back to the saddle shop bareback. I slapped on the saddle and saddle bags, and attached the scabbard into which I shoved my rifle.

Having decided to deliver my letter to Marie through Milt Warren, and knowing he would be arriving at the stockyards himself about now to buy some horses, I mounted, and rode back in the direction I had just come from. It didn't take me long to find him. He was forking hay to the horses he had just bought. Milt was the exact opposite of his wife. He was tall, thin, and whipcord tough from years of hard living on a Pennsylvania farm.

"Hello Matt," he said, forking over more hay to his horses. "Nice horse. Yours?"

"Yep."

"Mostly Morgan with a splash of Kentucky thoroughbred somewhere along the line. Am I right?"

"That's what the man who sold him to me said."

"Thought so," he said, putting down the pitchfork and leaning against the stall.

Reaching into my shirt pocket I pulled out the letter I had written to Marie the night before. "Mr. Warren, I'd appreciate if you'd give this to Marie," I said, handing him the letter.

Taking the letter, he asked, "You leavin'?"

"Yes," I said, my head bowed.

He studied me a bit longer, searching my face. "Taking the coward's way out, huh?"

Now ordinarily I would have been balling my fist up getting ready to fight for a comment like that. But this was a man whose family I had shared many a meal with around the campfire at night. And more than that, he was right. I was taking the coward's way out. So, keeping my eyes on the ground, I answered, "Yes sir, I guess I am."

"Son," he said, his tone softening. "I can guess what you're thinking. You're just gettin' started in life right now and a wife don't fit in your plans. And you figure to scoot on out of here and wait on a more convienent time to fall in love. Is that about it?"

I nodded.

"Well, Matt, love ain't a thing of convenience. If anything it's more a matter of an inconvenience. Same as children. When they decide to show up—they show up, no matter what. And have you given any thought as to how Marie is going to take you leaving without a proper goodbye?"

Well, I just stood there dumbfounded for a few seconds before I could answer. "No, I reckon not."

Walking away from the stall, he stuffed the letter back into my pocket. "Go back to the hotel, run off my old woman and the kids, and have a heart-to-heart talk with that girl. Lay your cards on the table. After all, this is the girl you are going to be spending the rest of your life with. You might as well start off honest with each other. It saves time and hurt feelings later on."

Milt was right. I did owe Marie a face-to-face explanation of how I felt and what I was afraid of. Shaking Mr. Warren's hand, I left with that very goal in mind.

Chapter Six
Marie's Kin

Having had the talk with Marie that Milt Warren had suggested, I had decided to stay in New Orleans and was having supper with the Warren family and Marie. My temporary "cold feet" proved to be the subject of interest for everybody that night. Mrs. Warren had made it clear that she thought I must certainly be some sort of a young fool to have even of thought of leaving Marie the way I had, and Milt, while more understanding than his wife, had told me that he was glad that I had come to my senses before Marie had left with them for Texas. In Texas there would be a shortage of women, and someone as beautiful as Marie would not go unmarried for very long. He also pointed out to Mrs. Warren that I was still just a kid who didn't know that living long enough to raise up my family would be all of the adventure that a man ever needed in life.

After supper was over and Mary Warren had decided that I had been raked over the coals enough for my lapse of judgment, the children were put to bed and the Warrens sat around the table making plans for the trip to Texas. Mr. Warren had bought a wagon and supplies and was planning on striking out for their new home in a couple of days.

The Warrens were excited about the trip but Marie had something else on her mind that night. That afternoon I had walked with Marie around the city and we had encountered a man and woman who she claimed reminded her of the fact that she had relatives in New Orleans. She said that the man reminded her so much of her father that she almost ran to him as soon as she saw him on the street. I had never met her father but when I looked at the woman who was walking beside him I got a real shock, for the woman looked like an older version of Marie. The woman I saw had black hair as did Marie but hers was streaked with gray and her face was beginning to develop a few wrinkles around the eyes, although she was making a valiant attempt to cover them up with some sort of face paint. But no amount of makeup could disguise what I saw in her eyes. At first I thought of it as hatred but later I would know it was pure evil.

Extending a gloved hand, the woman said, "Excuse my boldness, Miss, but may I ask you what your name might be?"

Marie told me that her father's words came back to her just then and she remembered how very much afraid of his family he had seemed to be. She remembered how he had told her to run if she ever met anyone who resembled either of them, and here she was in that very situation. But she said that since I was there she felt safe enough to take the woman's extended hand and say, "My name is Marie Laborteaux."

I could see the woman wince like someone had slapped her in the face and saw her look at her companion. The man and woman both stared at each other for a few seconds. And then, with an eyebrow raised, the woman asked, "Was your father's name Jean?" Marie gasped and her hand shot to her mouth but she soon recovered enough to answer with a very nervous "Yes."

The woman nodded to the man and for the first time, he spoke. "My dear, my name is Henri Laborteaux and this is my sister, Catherine. We are your aunt and uncle."

Nothing was said for several seconds with all of us just sort of looking at one another and wondering what was going to happen next. And then I said something that got Marie to dig her fingernails into my arm with such force that I flinched. "Marie, I can leave you to get better acquainted with your kin if you'd like." Now I know that from the way Marie had reacted in the first place that she had no desire to be around these people, but I was only trying to be polite. Fortunately, Marie could think faster than I could and said, "I have some things I have to help the Warrens with and I have to get back." And then turning to her aunt, she said, "I'm sure you understand."

"Of course, my dear," said her aunt. "But so we can get better acquainted I insist that you allow me to send a carriage to where you are staying tomorrow night to bring you to our home where we're having a party. That way we can spend the entire evening getting to know each other." And then, as an afterthought, she added, "You know, just the family catching up on what's new."

Marie's aunt was polite, but I sure caught what she meant by that: *"You ain't welcome, boy."* I could tell that Marie really didn't want to go to their home and was trying desperately to think of some graceful way of declining the invitation, but in the end she resigned herself to her fate and said, "Very well." And then she told what I was sure that polite folks would have called a fib. "It'll be nice to learn more about my father's family."

After giving her relatives the name of the hotel she was staying at so that they could send the carriage for her, we all nodded and smiled to one another and parted. And as I left I wondered why it was that neither of Marie's relatives had asked about her father. It seemed only natural to ask about kin that you hadn't seen in a long time. Well, maybe city folks were different when it came to kin.

My thoughts were brought back to the present by the sound of Milt Warren clearing his throat and speaking to Marie. "Matt told me about you meeting your kin. He also told me about the warning that your pa gave you concerning your relatives so I did some checking around town." Pausing to light his pipe, he continued, "Turns out the Laborteauxs are very rich. Their money comes from a silver mine that they own in Nevada. And it seems that at one time there was a lot more of their relatives sharing in the wealth of that mine for a time. But they all ended up dead or disappearing under what folks around here are calling mysterious circumstances."

"How'd Marie's aunt and uncle get the mine in the first place?" I asked.

"The mine was discovered by Marie's grandfather, Leon Laborteaux, who died shortly after returning to New Orleans. But before he died he'd drawn up a will that left everything he owned in equal shares to all of his family who could be found. It was about that time that a plague of strange illnesses and mysterious accidents started to happen to members of the Laborteaux family. I think that's probably why Marie's pa took off for the wilderness. Anyway, the upshot of the whole thing was the fact that Marie's aunt and uncle were the only two surviving relatives of Leon's who could be found—until now, that is."

"Does that mean that Marie owns part of that mine?" I asked.

"It sure does. It also means that Marie owns a third of everything her aunt and uncle own. That includes that fine

mansion that she's been invited to. Of course, taking pos-
sesion of what is rightfully hers is a different matter all
together; she could easily end up dead if she ain't careful.
In fact, I figure that her relatives will try to kill her no
matter what she does."

Marie sighed, folded her arms against the chill, and
asked Milt what he thought she should do. "The way I see
it you got two choices: run, or find a lawyer to fight for
you in court. You'll still have to keep looking over your
shoulder for killers as long as your aunt and uncle are alive
to hire them to try to kill you, but you'll certainly be able
to hire plenty of people to watch your back when you win
your share of the estate."

"But I don't have the kind of money needed to hire a
lawyer," protested Marie.

"I know," said Milt. "That's why I got the name of an
attorney here in town who will take your case on something
called a contingency basis. What that means is that he has
to win the case to get paid; seems to me that's the way all
lawyering ought to be done anyway."

None of us said anything for several minutes. It was
Marie's choice as to how she wanted to handle the situation. We could give advice, but none of us could make the
decision for her. If it had been me alone, I would have told
her kin to dig deep into their war chest, for I wasn't going
to be easy to kill. Finally Marie broke the silence by saying,
"I'm not interested in their money. All I want to do is raise
a family somewhere I can live in peace. And that's what I
plan to tell my aunt and uncle tomorrow night when I go
to their house. I'll even offer to sign a paper giving up all
my rights to the mine. That ought to satisfy them."

I had my doubts, but it was Marie's decision and I didn't
try to talk her out of it even though I was sure that she was
making a big mistake. So we all said good night to each

other and I headed for my room where I spent a good part of the night lying in bed thinking about how things could change at the drop of a hat. Here Marie was a poor orphan one day, the next day a rich heiress. But along with that wealth she finds some relatives willing to kill her for her share of it.

The next morning I was up early as usual. I had decided to appoint myself as Marie's personal bodyguard until she could afford to buy some of that high-priced hired help that Milt had talked about the night before.

Marie was busy with the final arrangements for her meeting with the Laborteauxs and fending off Mrs. Warren who was fussing over her like she was a child who was being sent off to her first day of school. They had one argument that I couldn't keep from laughing at. It concerned an alteration Marie wanted to make in the sleeve of the dress that she would be wearing that night.

Throwing up her hands in despair, Mrs. Warren said, "For goodness' sake, girl, I've never heard of such a thing in my life. Of all things, sticking a firearm up the sleeve of such a beautiful dress. Why . . . well, I've never heard of such a thing!"

Milt, hearing his wife's bellowing, stuck his head into the room, and when he heard about what Marie wanted to do, he said, "Good idea. Do it." Then he wisely backed out of the door, leaving Marie smiling and his wife to fume.

The carriage arrived at the appointed hour. I was standing in the shadows of a building with my horse at the ready. I hadn't been invited to the soiree but I was planning on being nearby if Marie needed my help. Two men were sitting atop the carriage and one dropped to the ground and opened the door for Marie. The light was pretty dim so I didn't get a real good look at those two men, but there was just something about them that told me that they didn't belong with the type of fancy rig they were driving.

It was pretty dark that night so I couldn't really tell which way they were heading, not that I would have known that much about where I was at anyway since I'd only been in New Orleans for a few days. But wherever it was that they were going, it sure seemed that they were taking a mighty roundabout route. And then the carriage stopped in a blind alley.

I saw both men jump from the carriage and heard their boots hitting the cobblestone as they walked back to Marie. I could see the driver light a cigar outside the coach door and for the first time I got a good look at him. If Marie had got a good look at him the way I was then I'm sure that she would have never gotten into the carriage for he had the kind of face that would have scared little children. A scar ran up his cheek to where an eyeball had once been located. And I couldn't even begin to guess his age or race.

Touching the brim of his high hat with his fingers, he said, "Evenin', Missy, I've got a message from the Laborteauxs." Slipping a thin, long-bladed dagger from his boot, he threw open the door and said, "They said to tell you that they don't intend to share their money with no white-trash whelp from Arkansas." He began to make his thrust and I knew I'd have to be quick as I began to draw, but a shot came from inside the coach and he fell backward into the street with a .41 caliber slug lodged between his eyes from Marie's derringer.

The second assassin had drawn a pistol and was approaching Marie, but he never walked more than two steps as the Colt bucked in my hand and ended his sorry life.

Riding up to the coach, I said, "Let's get out of here, Marie." Not being the kind of girl who had to be told something more than once, Marie jumped to the street where I pulled her up beside me and kicked my horse into a gallop. When we were what I considered to be a safe distance from where I was sure the law would be showing up soon, I slowed the horse to a walk and asked, "You all right, Marie?"

"I'm fine, but how did you know this was going to happen?"

"Didn't, but I figured that it might. I been following you ever since you left the hotel, and it wasn't easy the way they were driving either."

"I'm glad they didn't lose you."

I took a deep breath and said, "Well, Marie, what do you figure on doing now that you know for sure that your kin want you dead?"

"I don't know.

"Mind if I make a suggestion?" I asked.

"Please!"

"Let's go see that lawyer Mr. Warren told us about. You sign the papers for him to start working for you here and me and you can head West with the Warrens while things get wrung out here."

"Do you think I'll be any safer in Texas?" she asked.

"Well, at least you won't be in the same town your kin is living in. And from what I hear about Texas, a lot of it is wide-open country where it would be right hard for these big-city types to be sneakin' up on you."

Laughing, Marie said, "All right."

The name of the attorney that Marie hired was Phillip Lawson. And he had had trouble with the Laborteauxs before and was looking forward to doing battle with them in court again. All that had been required of Marie was her signature on a document giving Lawson power of attorney and she was free to leave with the Warrens for Texas. There was no gurantee that Marie would be safe, but she would be far away from her relatives and they would be having their hands full dealing with her lawyer.

When compared to the trip that I had taken down the river, following a wagon train was pretty tame. Milt Warren had been elected as wagon boss of the outfit and everything ran along like clockwork, with only one incident happening early along the way that would stick in my mind. But with all things considered, it was a pretty peaceful journey to the Hill Country.

Chapter Seven
The Hill Country

The cabins were going up fast and the ground was being cleared and made ready for spring planting next year. But Milt Warren was cautious. He said that while the soil was rich, it was also thin. Well suited for the grazing of cattle and such, but it couldn't be pushed too hard to make a crop year after year. He figured the smart thing to do was to use one section to grow a crop on for one year and to then let it rest or lie fallow for two years and give it a chance to regenerate itself. Back east they were calling such practices crop rotation. But what Milt wanted to use most of his land for was cattle production.

I marveled at his ability to think things through. Most of his neighbors were out to plant every square inch of their property every year in hopes of getting as much use out of the soil that they could. And when the soil wore out, they'd just move on. But that wasn't the Warrens' way. They figured on staying and putting down deep roots. And I pitied who or whatever tried to move them off what was theirs.

I had already witnessed an example of the strength of his determination. Two days out of New Orleans two men

wearing black suits and sporting badges came up to the
wagon train and allowed as how they intended to take Marie back to the city to stand trial for the murder of two of
the town's upstanding citizens. Warren had told them that
he was well aware of what had happened and that he had
no intention of handing over anybody. Then he told them
that he was of a mind to give anybody who was inclined
to take anybody off his train some lead to pack back to
Louisiana with them. And then he told them to git or draw.
I could tell that they dearly wanted to try, but Milt's hand
was resting on the butt of his Remington cap-and-ball pistol. And they hadn't missed the fact that they were surrounded by shotgun toting settlers with hard looks on their
faces.

Finally, they backed off and rode out with one of them
throwing a threat over his shoulder, "This ain't over. You
haven't heard the last of us, Warren!"

"For your sake it better be," replied Milt.

Several men laughed and I could see the two supposed
lawmen wince as if someone had laid a whip across their
backs.

The next day everybody saw the same two men on top
of a hill about five hundred yards away watching them. Milt
looked up at them and said, "Some people you can't tell
anything. You just have to flat-out show them that you
mean what you say."

Going to the back of his wagon, Warren pulled out a
deerskin scabbard and, unwrapping one end, pulled out a
45-70 Sharps rifle equipped with a vernier sight. Fishing
around in a box he pulled out a shell that was near the size
of a man's thumb. Working the lever, he dropped the round
into the chamber. Moving the sight up to the five-hundred-
yard mark, he walked around to the front of the wagon.
Warning everybody to get a good hold on their

horses, Milt rested the barrel of the heavy gun on some furs he had stacked on the tailgate and took aim in the direction of the two men in black.

One of those two men was wearing one of those bowler hats that folks were inclined to shoot off the heads of the dudes who wore them. The buffalo gun boomed and when the cloud of white smoke finally cleared, everyone could see that the bowler hat that had been setting on the man's head a few seconds earlier, had disappeared.

Folding down the sight, Warren laid the rifle on the floorboard of the wagon, looked up the hill and when he noticed that the two men had left, he said, "I reckon they went lookin' for that durn hat."

After I saw Milt in action and since we had gone for months without hearing from Marie's kin's hired killers, I figured it was safe enough for me to head out and find some work as a cowhand. After all, here I was in Texas with a saddle and a horse and instead of working cattle I was helping Milt Warren work his new farm or sitting on my hands waiting for a riding job to drop in my lap. So after telling everybody what I thought about the situation they all agreed that I should ride out and try to find some work with a cattle outfit. Of course, I hated to leave Marie and my friends but blast it, I'd been dreamin' of being a cowboy most of my life and here I was in Texas with the chance of a lifetime.

That night I packed my gear and said my good-byes. I promised Marie I would come back for her in a few month's time—hopefully with enough money for a wedding ring. This seemed to make her nice and happy enough. She understood a man had to go out into the world and prove himself before he settled down. The next morning I rode out in search of a job.

Chapter Eight
Texas

I had almost reached my lifelong goal of becoming a cow-puncher; I had the gear and I was in Texas. All I needed was a job. Right then I figured that I was about as close to paradise as I was ever going to get—not that everybody agreed with me on my opinion of the cowboy life, or for that matter, Texas as being some sort of paradise. I remember one man telling me that Texas was only known for three things: being hot, dry, and worst of all, full of Texans.

That night at camp the horse I'd named Bluegrass in honor of his Kentucky roots munched on some hillside grass while I ate some of the fish I'd caught in a small creek. I'd noticed what appeared to be somebody riding mighty hard on my trail that day, but it didn't seem like he was trying to be sneaky about it or nothing like that. It just looked like he wanted to catch up to me in a real bad way. And he was having a hard time getting the job done with me astride of my big horse, for Bluegrass really liked to stretch out those long legs and eat up trail. So I decided to make an early camp to let whoever was trying to over-take me catch up. But since I didn't know the intentions of the man following me, I slipped into the shadows after I finished eating to wait for him.

I didn't have long to wait, for within ten minutes, a man trailing another horse came galloping into my camp.

"Coltrane! Matt Coltrane! Where you at?"

Recognizing the shouting man as Caleb Jensen, one of Rink's men, I stepped into the light. "Hello, Caleb. What brings you to Texas?"

It was an old joke but I suppose Jensen just couldn't resist saying, "One tired horse." And then, pushing back his hat, he said, "Rink sent me after you and I've been chasing you and that blasted fast horse of yours for three long hard days."

"Well, light and set. I've got coffee on and some fresh-caught fish along with beans and bacon."

"Thanks," he said, dismounting and digging out his eating tools from his mess kit. Pouring coffee into his cup, I took his plate and filled it with fish and beans.

I could see that he had been riding hard and was hungry so I didn't start pestering him with questions right off. I knew he would get around to telling me what he was supposed to when his belly got full.

As it turned out, he was hungrier than I had been and he wolfed the food down, barely stopping to chew it. Seeing that I had noticed how hungry he was, he said, "Been living on jerky for three days. When I stopped to rest during that time, I was just too tired to cook anything up so I just been riding, sleeping, and chewing on dried meat."

"Why two horses?"

"So I could travel faster. I rode one hard for a while, then switched to the other one. But the way you travel, I needed a whole remuda."

"What in the world did Mr. Rink think was so important for you to almost kill two horses?"

"To offer you a job."

"Hmm. I would have thought after the way I left town, Mr. Rink would have been too mad to think about hiring me back."

"He was put out some about the way you took off without talking things over with him, but he figures that you are still a kid who gets ideas into his head and just has to go traipsing off like some blasted fool. So he sent me after you to tell you about the offer."

"What's the job?" I asked, wondering if I would be told what we would really be doing this time.

"The U.S. Army wants us to deliver several wagonloads of rifles to a company of soldiers stationed near San Antonio. John said I was to tell you that you wasn't to be employed as a hunter this time, but as a scout."

"San Antonio? That's right near the Hill Country, ain't it?"

"Sure is."

Thinking about how well my good luck was holding out, I asked, "What about the pay?"

"Same as the rest of us. Fifty a month and found."

It wasn't a real hard decision to make. I had the choice of traveling through dangerous country by myself or going with a large, well-armed party of men who would feed me and pay me fifty dollars a month. And best of all, I would be heading in the direction I had already decided to go. I definitely had to have a talk with Rink about going to work for him full-time.

"We'll start back at first light," I said and walked back to my bed and rolled up into my blankets.

We met the wagon train at noon. Bluegrass had proven his worth once again. We had ridden hard, with Caleb switching mounts several times, but he couldn't keep up

with me no matter how hard he rode. And when we arrived
all three of the horses were well lathered.

Stepping down from Bluegrass, I strode stiffly over to
Rink and stuck out my hand. "Howdy, Mr. Rink, understand you have a job for me."

Grabbing my hand, he slapped me on the back. "Sure
do, son, but first you better fill up some. You'll be headin'
out as soon as we finish noonin'."

Walking over to the fire, I filled a cup with trail coffee
so strong it could have floated a horseshoe and filled my
plate with beans, salt pork, and some kind of biscuit. Being
afraid of insulting the cook, I didn't ask what kind of bread
it was. I decided the only thing I should open my mouth
for was to stick food in it.

Joining me, Rink said, "You know, Matt, I been thinking
awful serious about tying a cow bell around your neck the
next time we reach the end of the trail so I won't have to
be sending Jensen off to find you again."

"No need for that," I said around a mouthful of beans.
"I don't think you'll have that problem from now on. I
think you will always know where I can be found."

Reaching into my pocket, I handed him the letter I had
written. "Would you see to it that that letter gets posted as
soon as possible?"

Seeing who the letter was addressed to, he smiled and
said, "I hope she will still let you work for me."

"So do I," I said in all honesty. But if for some reason
she didn't, Rink would have to find a new man. For now,
I knew what was really important and I wouldn't risk losing
her again.

"Exactly what is it you want me to do, Mr. Rink? Caleb
said something about me being a scout."

"That's exactly what I want you to do, Matt. I want you
to ride a mile or more ahead of the train and keep an eye

out for trouble. If you see something wrong, I want you to high-tail it back here and warn us. There's been reports of Kiowas, and bandits robbing people all along the trail. And given the nature of the cargo I'm carrying, I don't want to end up arming a bunch of thieves with better firearms than they may already have."

Throwing the dregs of my coffee on the ground, I said, "Well, I might as well start earning my keep."

Pointing to the remuda, Rink said, "Throw your saddle on that roan over there and give your horse a rest. I brought along plenty of mounts so there's no reason to overwork any one horse."

Bluegrass wasn't feeling any ill effects from all the traveling we had been doing, but I didn't figure a nice break from carrying me over the road for a while would do him any harm. But he got downright restless when he saw me saddle that old roan. And if a horse can have his feelings hurt, I believe his were.

Forking that roan in a northerly direction, I rode hard until I was about two miles from the train. I figured that to be about the farthest I could be from the group and still be able to give them advance warning by firing off some shots.

I kept up a nice easy pace that I figured matched the speed of the wagons. The rest of the day was so peaceful that the only danger I was in was from falling asleep in the saddle and falling from my horse. And finding a place to camp didn't pose much of a problem, for at the end of the day, I found a perfect spot. The camp could be made by a stream in an open field concealed by two wooded hills that would hide us but still give us a good view of the trail. I rode a mile further on to scout out the territory. Noticing a narrow road to the right of the trail, I rode south, planning to follow it for a short distance out of idle curiosity. About a quarter mile from the main trail I found an abandoned farmhouse and barn. There was an old wooden bridge leading to the barn. So far it had been a pretty boring day and the prospect of poking around in an old abandoned barn looked to be about the only excitement I was going to get so I kicked that old roan in the side and started toward the bridge.

Suddenly I heard something whistling through the air and slam into my saddle near my leg. Looking down, I saw a feathered shaft sticking out of my saddle. My head snapped up when I heard a war whoop and I saw an Indian fifty feet to my right notching another arrow.

Slipping the thong from the Colt's hammer, I pulled the six-gun and leveled it at the Kiowa. The hammer of my gun dropped a split second before he released the taught bowstring. The Colt bucked in my hand and the Indian folded as his arrow went wide of its mark.

I surely wanted to turn that horse and run it full out back up that road to the main trail, but I didn't know how many weapons would be pointed at my back. As far as I knew I could be surrounded. And they could just be waiting for me to whirl that roan around and present my back as a target. And my pa had always told me that the thing to do when you were surrounded and had no hope of getting out alive, was to charge right into the enemy line. He said he had seen that kind of action carry the day more than once.

Figuring that no one would expect me to do it, I kicked that old roan in the ribs and ran it toward the barn. Another Kiowa ran from under the bridge with his bow drawn and loosed an arrow at me. I chopped down with my .44 and fired. My bullet took him in the chest and his arrow sliced through the side of my neck, causing warm blood to flow in a stream down the side of my throat.

Crossing the bridge, I took a 45-70 slug from a Sharps buffalo gun low down on my left side that exited out my back. The Indian who had fired that old rifle was a hundred yards in front of me trying to load another of those large shells into its breech. That first slug had hurt me enough to encourage me to do my best to make sure that Kiowa didn't get off another shot.

I started shooting at him as fast as I could pull the trigger. My first shot kicked up dust at his feet and made him so nervous that he gave up on trying to reload the piece and started to run for the cover of some nearby trees. My next two shots hurried him along but did no damage to him that I could see.

My Colt was empty so I dropped it back into my holster, and figuring that I was in for some hard, fast riding, I secured the thong around the hammer. There was a narrow trail on the left leading away from the homestead, so leaning forward to present a smaller target, I urged my horse into a gallop. I'd covered about a mile when the roan stumbled and started to go down. Kicking free of the stirrups, I hit the ground and rolled.

Regaining my feet, I walked over to my fallen mount and discovered that the arrow had gone deeper into the roan than I had at first thought. It appeared as if the shaft had penetrated the horse's lungs. It was a miracle that my mount had carried me as far as it had.

I'd heard it said that when it rains it pours. And I was beginning to see the truth in that old saw. For there I was with two bleeding wounds, a dead horse lying there with my rifle pinned beneath it where I couldn't get at it, and I could hear the hoofbeats of several horses coming up the trail in pursuit. It would have taken a real gambler to buck the odds stacked up against my surviving the next few minutes. But there wasn't nothing left but for me to try it.

Back about fifty feet there was a hill at the edge of the trail. Running over to it, I hid behind a tree and waited for my pursuers. It was a desperate gamble, but I figured to ambush them when they rounded the corner and before they could see my dead horse and start wondering where I was.

But first, I needed to reload my empty pistol—fast. Opening the loading gate, I found the empty chamber I always let my hammer rest against and filled it with a cartridge from by belt loop. Shucking a shell and filling an empty chamber one at a time I managed to load two more rounds before the Kiowas rounded the corner.

There were three of them. And each one of them carried a weapon. Their horses spooked when I jumped from behind that tree and yelled. One horse reared, dropping his rider to the ground. Another horse skidded to a halt, throwing his rider over his head. The last man, riding the pinto, kept his seat but dropped his buffalo rifle when his mount started sunfishing.

The first one was armed with a lance and as soon as he could get to his feet, he started to lunge at me with it. A quick shot from the Colt ended his try. The second Kiowa was coming after me with a tomahawk, but he didn't make it very far carrying the lead bullet I put in his chest. The third one had regained control of the pinto and was riding away fast, hanging from the horse's side using its body as a shield. Knowing that I couldn't chance giving him the opportunity to sneak back while I was in such a weakened condition, I had to finish the fight now. Thumbing back the hammer on the Colt, I fired my last round at the pinto, instantly dropping the pony.

Tumbling head over heels, he quickly came to his feet and ran toward me with his knife held low, with the cutting edge up.

Knowing I could never reload the Colt fast enough, I dropped it to the ground and clawed for the derringer in my shirt pocket. The Kiowa was ten feet from me when I fired the shot. Taking the hit and showing no effect, he stabbed out at me as we came together. We fell to the ground, grappling with each other. He had positioned himself to bring the knife down in an arc, driving it into my chest when I touched off the second and final round in the little pistol. The slug entered under his chin and drove into his brain pan, killing him instantly.

I was so weak from the blood loss caused by my wounds that I could barely muster enough strength to push his lifeless body off me.

Looking around me I found my pistol a couple of feet away. Fearing that I would pass out from a loss of blood and desperately wanting water from the canteen under my dead horse were my major concerns at the time, but I put both those concerns down as being nowhere near as important as getting my Colt reloaded.

It was a struggle but I managed to get six fresh cartridges into the gun. And then, I passed out.

Chapter Nine
The Bounty Hunter

My trip back to consciousness was a slow one. It felt as if I was swimming through a thick fog. The first thing I became aware of was a rocking motion. Then there was the sounds of horses and trace chains. Opening my eyes to narrow slits, I became aware of a yellow, muted light. It was canvas. I was riding in a covered wagon. And then I heard the voice coming from the front of the wagon.

"He's awake!"

The wagon stopped. The canvas flap at the back opened and John Rink crawled in.

"How you doin', Matt?"

My throat hurt and was so dry that when I spoke it sounded like a stranger was forming words in my mouth.

"Water. I need a drink."

Looking at the driver, Rink said, "We'll noon here. Bring water and get the cook to heat up that soup. And have him bring a plate of beans and coffee for me. I'll take my meal with Matt in here."

A canteen was passed back to Rink. Holding it to my mouth, he said, "Sip it slow. We've got a broth the cook made up for you, and coffee if you want it."

85

Although I wanted to gulp that water down as fast as I could, I followed his instructions and sipped it slowly. As my thirst began to ease, Rink helped me into a sitting position. Soon a cup of warm broth was passed back to me and Rink helped ease me to a sitting position where I could sip the liquid. I had no idea that I was as hungry as I was. But the first sip of that broth fired my appetite and I fairly inhaled the rest of it in record time. Removing the cup from my lips, Rink handed the empty cup to the man who had brought him his beans and coffee. Instructing the man to refill my cup with more broth, he handed me the other cup of coffee the cook had sent for me, and then started to stir the beans in his own plate in preparation to start shoveling them into his mouth.

"What about some solid food?" I managed to say, pointing at his plate of beans.

Laughing, he passed me his plate, and then leaned back against a sack of flour to drink his coffee. Between mouthfuls, I asked, "What happened? How'd I get here?"

"We tracked you, Matt. You really had yourself quite a fracas back there. And it weren't no big job we had to find you. Everywhere you went you left dead bodies. We counted five all told."

"Who were they?"

"Kiowa. I've been hearing rumors about how they been teaming up with some renegade whites around here to rob and kill folks traveling. Sort of like what the Comanches and Comancheros did. We figure that their white partners are still around somewheres so we all been riding real cautious the last few days."

"Days? Just how long have I been out?"

"Three days. We loaded you onto this wagon three days ago when we found you passed out, and brought you back to camp where Caleb Jensen tried his hand at stitching you up. You'd lost a lot of blood and some of the men were betting on whether or not you would live. You might be interested to know, that all of the men who rode down the Mississippi with us took all bets from my new employees that you would beat the angel of of death."

Laughing, I said, "Durn happy that I didn't disappoint any of the ones who bet on me."

"No happier than they are, I imagine. You see, the new men gave them five-to-one odds that you would never wake up."

We both laughed. And then, remembering my gear, I asked, "What about my rifle and saddle?"

"We picked them up. As a matter of fact, your head's been restin' on your saddle the last three days, and I personally cleaned and reloaded both of your pistols. They will be ready for you as soon as you're in shape to ride again. Although I don't think that will be for some time. It'll probably be days before you're fit to ride. And since you've already done more than enough to earn your keep for this trip, you might as well sit back and enjoy the scenery."

Taking my plate and cup, Rink dropped to the ground and mounted his horse. Giving the order to move out, the wagon I was in began to roll once again. Lying back there by myself, it didn't take me long to get restless. The food and coffee seemed to perk me up and soon I was sitting up front with the driver who just happened to be the man who patched me up, Caleb Jensen. Moving up to the seat beside him, I wondered how much money he had just won from my having woke up.

"You know, Coltrane, when you find a bunch of bandits, you don't have to take 'em all on by yourself," he said, grinning a gap-toothed smile.

"I tried to talk them into waiting and letting the rest of

you old boys in on the fun, but for some reason they was in a hurry and didn't want to wait."

Chuckling, Jensen slapped the reins across the horse's backs and said, "Git on up there!"

It was two full days before Rink let me take to the saddle again. Relenting then only because Jensen begged him to, saying that my constant complaining about being cooped up was going to drive us both off the deep end if I wasn't allowed to go back to work.

While I was back as scout, there had been some changes made while I was taking my forced vacation. Instead of there being only one scout a couple of miles from the train, there were now two men pulling that duty. The first man rode about two miles from the wagons while a second man rode a mile behind him staying in sight of the train at all times. Rink said to think of it as insurance. That way the scout would never be out of sight. In general, it was a good plan. But he failed to take into account human nature. And that old saying about curiosity killing the cat. For on that day I was the second scout and I was watching Dell Brooks about a mile ahead of me on point. To his right I could see a road leading to the remnants of a town. Some people called them ghost towns. It was then that Dell did what I would have done. He rode toward the town to look it over. And while I would have been happy to join him in his exploration, I knew that if I disappeared from Rink's view that everything would grind to a halt while someone rode out to see why I wasn't where I was supposed to be. So, curbing my youthful enthusiasm, I continued to plod along, keeping pace with the train.

A couple of minutes later I heard the shot coming from the town. Knowing I would be followed, I urged Bluegrass into a gallop. Skidding to a halt in front of the saloon, I could see Dell's body lying on the sidewalk. His gun was missing and his pockets had been pulled inside out.

Fighting the urge to go to my friend, I forced my horse to back up. I had moved about twenty feet when a man rose from the roof of the saloon and trained the twin barrels of a shotgun on me. It was close, but I managed to draw and fire before he got settled steady enough to pull the triggers, causing him to fling the shotgun outward and roll off the roof and fall to the ground with a heavy thump.

Hearing a board creak behind me, I whirled my mount around in time to see a man disappear in a cloud of white smoke from the rifle he had fired at me. The bullet hit me low down on my right side, almost unseatintg me with its force. Not being able to see my attacker, I fired three quick shots at where I figured him to be and was gladdened to hear the body fall.

I felt the wind from a heavy slug pass less than an inch from my skull as I turned Bluegrass up the town street. I could see a grizzled old man trying desperately to load a thumb-sized shell into an old Sharps. Firing my last shot, I hit the breech of that old weapon, causing a chunk of hot metal to fly upward, cutting a deep gash in his cheek. I didn't think that jagged piece of iron was going to do much to improve his looks. Especially since he didn't have much to work with to begin with.

Holstering the Colt, I shucked the Winchester from its scabbard. Covering him with the rifle, I told him to lie face down in the dirt.

Waiting for a few seconds to make sure nobody else was going to pop out of the woodwork, I dismounted and went into my saddlebags to get some rawhide strips to bind the man with part of a face.

Walking back up the street to Dell, I checked to see if he was still alive. He was still breathing but he was in pretty rough shape. He managed to rouse himself enough to tell me what had happened. Helping him to sit up, I listened to his story. It seems that after riding up to the saloon three men came out and asked him to join them in a friendly little card game. But Dell had been around way too long to get into a card game with three strangers in a deserted town. So he made his excuses and was turning to leave when one of them just up and shot him.

"I was watching them real close, Matt, but one of them managed to work around the side of me and get off a shot before I could even touch the handle of my gun. Got me in the side," he said, lifting his shirt to show me the wound.

Checking it over, I could see that it was a clean wound with the bullet having gone clean through. "Don't look too bad, Dell. Only danger from it is the chance it might get infected. But I got something to keep that from happening," I said, and walked over to my saddle bags, where I removed a small jar of salve Rink had given me. He'd bought it off of an Indian, and he'd seen it work wonders at treating cuts and all other kinds of wounds. I didn't know what it was made of, but I was willing to give it a try.

Walking back over to my friend, I asked if he was ready for me to try my hand at doctoring.

"Sure, but don't you think it might be a good idea to patch yourself up first before you start trying to work on me?" he asked, pointing at my blood-soaked shirt.

Looking down at my right side, I said, "Dang it, Texas is sure hard on new shirts." Then lifting the shirt to see how bad I was hurt, I said, "The bullet dug out a row deep enough to plant corn in, but I think I can get by with the salve for now. Later, I'll check with Caleb to see if he wants to stitch it up a mite."

Taking a big gob of the greasy salve, I massaged it deep into my wound, wincing with the pain. Tucking my shirt back into my pants, I reached back into the jar to get some more salve and work on Dell's wound.

Holding up his hand, Dell said, "Just hold on there a minute, son. If you plan on doing to me what you just did to yourself, I'll be a needin' some pain-killer."

"Don't have any," I said.

"I do," he said. "Check in my right saddle bag."

Doing as he asked, I rumbled around in there until I came out with a pint of grade A skull-buster. Putting the bottle to his lips, he downed half of the brown liquid. After a couple of minutes he looked up at me and said, "I'm ready, go ahead on."

Apparently the whiskey worked, for I could tell as I rubbed the salve in the deep wound he was feeling no pain. I had just finished and was tucking in his shirt when Rink and four other men rode into the ghost town.

Dismounting, Rink walked over to the saloon and said, "I don't know what in the world I'm going to do with you, Coltrane. It seems that every time I let you out loose by yourself, you get yourself shot full of holes. And now you've gone and got Brooks shot up too."

"Well, I was just checking up on Dell here, when these three jokers started shooting at me. They didn't give me much of chance to talk things over with them."

"Blast it, Coltrane! If you had bothered to follow my orders in the first place, you might not have gotten shot at all. The reason I kept the scouts in sight was so that no one would have to face trouble by himself. I believe you think I did it so that you could get to where the action is faster. Son, if you don't start developing a little caution, you ain't never going to live long enough to hear anybody call you grandpa!"

He looked me over to see if he could tell if I was taking what he had to say seriously. Apparently he wasn't satisfied, for the next thing he said was, "Tommorow you take Jensen's place driving a wagon." And seeing that I was about to protest, he said, "Before you open your mouth, I think you should know that I'm just about at the point where I'm ready to take that gun off of you and beat the living tar out of you until you learn who the bull of the woods is in this outfit."

Standing there with his legs spread out and his fists balled at his side, he asked, "Got anything to say, boy?"

I'd just finished a fight where I had killed two men and ruined another, but at no time did I feel I was in the danger I was in then, facing that man. Not that I would have, but I would have been afraid to shoot him for fear of just making him madder.

"All right, first thing in the morning I want your butt planted on a wagon seat and I don't want to hear one word of complaint," Rink said, and then stomped away.

Letting out a breath, I said, "Whew, he sure was mad. I hope he simmers down some. Be mighty rough in camp with a boss that mad."

"Don't let his manner fool you, Matt. He thinks of all of us as his children. Even the ones older than him. And what he said to you was nothing more than him threatening to take you out behind the woodshed."

"Sure wouldn't want to make too many trips out behind the woodshed with him when he was that mad," I said, helping Brooks to his feet and walking with him over to the wagon brought up to transport him back to the train.

By nightfall Rink had calmed down. Especially after Brooks had explained that he was the first one to break the rule about always remaining in sight and that I had only rode in trying to help him. Of course that shifted the blame over to Brooks, but Rink had already expended all his rage at me, and since Dell had some serious wounds, Rink let it pretty much go. Although he did ask Dell what he had been using for brains lately.

After supper Rink walked up to where Jensen was sewing up my latest wound. "How's the wound, Matt?"

"Not too bad. It's sore and I figure it to be stiff for a few days and I'll have to be careful about how I move, but it shouldn't give me too much trouble."

"Good," he said, squatting by the fire. "Dell and I talked it over and we both figure you ought to have the outlaws' guns and horses. I figure they'll probably bring about three hundred dollars. Of course, they are the property of outlaws and might have been stolen, so you best be careful about where you try to sell them. You wouldn't want to try to sell a stolen horse to the man who had it stolen from him. Things could turn nasty in a big hurry. We'll be in Tyler tomorrow. I suggest we leave the horses and weapons with the law and let them be sold in that town and give anybody who might have a claim on them have a chance to prove ownership. How's that sound to you, Matt?"

"Sounds fine," I answered.

Reaching into a vest pocket, Rink pulled out three folded sheets of paper. "When we went through the dead men's pockets we found these on one of them. Seems he was right proud that him and his two compadres were wanted men."

Placing the three wanted posters in front of me he said, "The total amount for the three of those owl hoots comes to fifteen hundred dollars."

I suppose it was lucky that I was sitting down, because news like that could have easily put me down. Sitting there with my mouth open, it took me a while to grasp what Rink was saying.

"There's a sheriff in Tyler and a U.S. Marshal who works out of that town. I know them both, so I should be able to smooth things over for you and get you all set up to collect those rewards. That way you can go on with us to San Antonio. Of course, I'm assuming you are still going on to the end of trip. You do know that with all that money you don't have to go anywhere you don't want to. Heck! You don't even have to stay in Texas if there's somewhere else you want to be."

I was still kind of loopy from the news, but I did manage to say, "Of course, I'm going on to San Antonio. Why, I haven't even been on a trail drive yet."

"Son, with the kind of cash you'll have after Tyler, you can buy your own herd and drive them anywhere you want to. And you can play cowboy till your plumb sick of chasing cows," said Rink.

Later that night I thought about what Rink had said. He was certainly right. By my figures I would have around two thousand dollars. And with the price of cattle in Texas being as low as two dollars a head, I should be able to put together a fair-sized herd and drive them up north to where I had been hearing that they were selling as high as twenty dollars a head. And there was the possibility that if I could put together a large enough herd, I could settle on some land up north and start my own ranch. It was a gamble in that I could lose the entire herd and be back where I started. But having lived seventeen years on a farm with my parents, taking a gamble wasn't anything new to me. For although my pa didn't hold with gambling with cards and dice, he was always betting against the weather, bugs, and crop prices that had a tendency to head south at a run. The only difference in my case would be that instead of gambling on beans and corn, I'd be betting on cattle.

The sheriff of Tyler was a man named Frank Baldwin. He was a tall man of forty or so who sported a long droopy moustache, and wore his gun cross-draw fashion. His belly he wore over his belt. And from the way he was looking

at me after I told him what my business with him was, I
figured he would have liked to have drawn his long-
barreled Colt and rapped me on the side of the head with
it.

"In my opinion, you durn bounty hunters are just about
as low as they come," said Baldwin.

Rink, seeing how things were about to shape up, said,
"Hold on there, Sheriff. Coltrane's no bounty hunter. He
works for me as a scout. He only ran into those men when
he was doing his job. He didn't even know they had boun-
ties on their heads until I told him. And I didn't know it
either until I found those wanted posters when I searched
for the dead men's bodies."

The sheriff took a long, measuring look at me before he
said, "An accidental run-in, with them knowing you were
coming and you end up plugging all three of them, and
then you end up rich in the process. I guess that makes you
the luckiest man I ever met. Or the biggest liar."

Well, I was already mad, but now I was ready to make
that sheriff eat that long-barreled gun of his. So, lifting my
shirt to show him the bullet wound I had gotten from the
fight as a souvenir, I said, "If you'll notice that bullet
wound is in the front the same as all the ones in those
outlaws. I'm not in the habit of shooting people in the
back!"

The sheriff wasn't satisfied with my explanation. To his
way of thinking, Wyatt Earp couldn't out-fight three men
in a straight-up gunfight, let alone some kid take on three
men from ambush and come out ahead.

"I'll send a few wires and make some inquiries around
town. I need to make sure that those bodies outside are the
same ones listed on these wanted posters," he said, pointing
to the circulars Rink had laid on his desk.

Starting to worry, I looked over at Rink who I knew

couldn't wait around town for this indolent sheriff to verify the identities of the outlaws we had brought in.

Glancing at his pocket watch, Rink asked, "How long you figure to take doing all that?"

The sheriff smiled, enjoying the predicament he was about to put me in. Leaning back in his chair, he said, "Oh, it shouldn't take more than a month or so."

Looking disgusted, Rink turned to me and said, "Matt, let's see about getting our hands on some rock salt and try our luck at salting down those bodies until we hit a town where we can find a lawman who doesn't have sawdust for brains."

Rink had turned to walk out of the office and I was about to follow him when Baldwin sprang from his chair and started to draw his pistol. "Now hold on there," he said. But he choked off the rest of what he was about to say when he saw the muzzle of my .44 staring him in the face. Regaining his composure, he continued to bluster, but he kept his hand well away from the grip of his Colt.

"You can't take those bodies out of town," said Baldwin.

"Why not?" asked Rink.

"Because I'm the sheriff, and I . . . well, I have to make sure that those are the men you claim they are," he said.

"No need for that," said a gravely voice to my right.

Glancing to my right, I saw a tall man around fifty years old who held his hands out in front of him to show me that he carried no weapons. But a well-worn Smith & Wesson pistol hung at his side and a U.S. Marshal's badge was pinned to his chest.

"You can put the pistol away, son. If the sheriff gets out of hand again, you can rap him on the head with your Colt. He ain't really worth the price of a bullet anyway."

Holstering my weapon, I watched as the lawman walked across the room, took a chair, and sat astraddle of it.

"My name's Red Davis. I'm the marshal for this area and sometimes up in the Cherokee nation. Now, what seems to be the trouble?"

The sheriff started to speak, but Davis silenced him with a wave of his hand. And then indicating me with his thumb, he said, "Let's hear your side of the story, son."

Jumping right in, I explained about what had happened. I tried to gloss over the gun play, but Rink would have none of that, for he had also been insulted by the sheriff's questioning of my ability. And before he was finished adding to my narrative, Wild Bill Hickcock would have been honored to have cleaned and oiled my weapons to hear him tell it.

Listening to my story, and Rink's embellishments, without interruption, Davis nodded to the sheriff and said, "Baldwin, you go have a drink; I'll handle this."

The sheriff stood up and walked out the door without uttering a word. It was obvious that whatever dispute those two had ever had over who was in charge, had been resolved in the marshal's favor. Later, I found out that Davis had almost beat the younger sheriff to death with his fists in a dispute over a Mexican prisoner.

Walking over to Baldwin's desk, Davis opened the top drawer and rifled around in it until he came out with three wanted posters. Laying them on top of the desk, he compared them to the posters Rink and I had. Looking them over, he said, "I checked the two bodies outside and the prisoner you brought in. They match up. And I recognize all of them. I've been on their trail for the last three months. They had a real bad habit of teaming up with renegade Indians and robbing and killing folks all over the territory. I'm real happy that you put an end to their careers. As far as I'm concerned, the people in this state owe you every penny of that reward money."

Comparing the two sets of posters, I noticed that the amounts of the rewards didn't match up. Davis, taking notice of my confusion, said, "Those posters of yours are old ones. The ones I dug out of the desk are the most recent. They've been hard at work robbing and killing folks, so the rewards got higher." Looking the circulars over and doing some quick arithmetic in his head, Davis said, "I figure it comes to about three thousand dollars all told."

We all signed some papers. My signature said I was who I said I was. Rink's signature said I was who I said I was and Davis's signature signified that we both could write our names.

After all the signing was over, Davis walked us over to the bank and Rink and I rode out of Tyler, Texas, with me being three thousand dollars richer.

The marshal agreed to sell the outlaw's horses and gear and send the money to a bank in San Antonio, where I could draw on it. There shouldn't be any problem. After all, I would be riding into that town a very rich man.

Chapter Ten
The Ten Percent Condition

John Rink had signed on for a one-man courier job and that left his crew free to do as they pleased for several months. The result was that we weren't in San Antonio but a few hours when all business was completed and the crew scattered to the four winds to visit family and friends. Well, about everybody took off. Brooks and Jensen were both in their late forties and were looking for a place to settle down with their families. So they bought into my dream and signed on as cattle hands. And I was glad to get them since they had spent their youth trailing cattle up north. They had both worked for some famous cattlemen.

I certainly lacked experience and only had the most general of plans. I had heard that cattle were selling for about two dollars a head in Texas and going for as high as twenty dollars a head in Kansas. It didn't take much of a businessman to see the opportunity that was staring me in the face. Jensen said it came down to only two things that a cattleman needed—money and guts.

At two dollars a head I figured to buy around a thousand head. Then taking into account the cost of a chuck wagon, a remuda, and other supplies, not to mention the cost of paying wages and expenses for three or more months, I figured to be broke when I reached my destination. It was the biggest gamble of my life.

Caleb recommended that I hire three more hands. And since I would only be paying thirty a month, I had to be real careful about who I hired because Jensen had told me that at that price I'd be hiring the youngest and greenest of cowboys. I also had to be picky about who I hired, for I was planning to settle on some land up north and raise cattle. And with that in mind I would like to keep my trail hands on to work my ranch.

That was my intention as I sat at the table drinking a beer with Caleb Jensen that day. I'd been watching the customers in the saloon for about half an hour when I noticed my first prospect. I figured him to be a man of about twenty whose face was beginning to take on a leather toughness from long hours spent under the hot Texas sun. The other thing I noticed about him was his height. It didn't look like he stood much over five feet four inches tall. Remembering how cruel children could be, and how stupid adults were, it must have been tough having to deal with the taunts that must have come his way. And that he probably answered to the name of Shorty.

Shorty, as I began to think of him, bellied up to the bar and ordered a beer. The cowboy to his right looked down on him and snickered. I had been watching that cowboy and had even considered hiring him, but had given up on him as I watched him continually pouring drinks of hard whiskey down his throat.

"You sure that you're old enough to order a man's drink, little boy?" asked the cowboy who had snickered. Shorty took his beer and walked to the back of the room. The cowboy at the bar was put out by what he took to be an affront to his dignity. Of course, the thought that he might have insulted Shorty didn't even cross his mind.

Staggering over to Shorty's table, he stood in front of the short cowhand, weaving, barely able to remain standing. "What's the matter, boy? You got mud in your ears or somethin'? I'm askin' you if you are old enough to drink. 'Cause you don't look tall enough to be much over ten years old to me."

Shorty looked up at the cowboy and said, "I'm old enough, friend. And now that I've answered your question, I'm wondering if you'd answer one for me?"

The cowboy's mind was pretty fogged with the whiskey but he did manage to say, "Huh?"

Smiling, Shorty said, "That's two questions you've asked, but I've only got the one."

Standing there, confused, the cowboy just stared at Shorty. He was vaguely aware of the fact that he was being made fun of but couldn't think of how to handle the situation. While he was thinking the situation over, Shorty continued. "My question is this. Suppose we fight and I whip you. How do you suppose people around town would treat you after that? And if you was to beat me, people would say you was only man enough to take on a runt. So the way I see it, you lose either way."

The cowboy's name was Jake Collins and basically he was a good kid. But he was young and had had too much to drink. Whiskey sometimes led a man down a mighty rocky path. But at seventeen, the alchohol hadn't had time enough to cloud young Collins's mind the way it would have an older man's, so Shorty's words sank in.

Putting out a hand to steady himself on a nearby chair, he used his other hand to tip his hat to Shorty, turned, and walked unsteadily out the bat-wing doors.

Motioning to Jensen, I walked over to Shorty's table.

"My name's Matt Coltrane, and this here's Caleb Jensen," I said, indicating Caleb with my thumb. "Mind if we sit and talk a while?"

"Sit," he said, motioning to a couple of chairs.

"Might you be looking for a job?" I asked.

"Mister, this is Texas, everybody and his dog is looking for a way to make more money. Me included."

"Well, I plan to put together a herd of longhorns down here and drive them up north where I plan to sell most of them. But I also plan to keep enough of them to start me a fair-sized ranch where the graze is good. And if things work out on the trail, I plan on offering the men who go along on the drive permanent employment once we get to where we're going."

"Cattle, depending on type and quality, are selling from two to ten dollars a head, in Texas. How big a herd are you planning to put together and where do you figure to drive them to?"

"My plan is to pay two dollars a head and drive them to Dodge City, Kansas when I gather a thousand head."

Shorty rolled himself a smoke and looked thoughtfully toward the bar. "You got yourself a remuda yet . . . or a chuck wagon?"

"No."

Lighting the cigarette, Shorty asked, "How many hands you got?"

"I plan to run a crew of five. I already have two, three if you hire on. I need to get two more hands."

Taking a drag on the cigarette, he blew smoke toward the ceiling and said, "I work for a man by the name of Frank Carpenter and I think he may have exactly what your looking for."

We talked for a bit longer and he gave me directions to Frank Carpenter's ranch. And as we parted I asked him for his name. He said it was Lou Costas, but everybody knew him as Shorty.

That evening I rode out to the ranch with Brooks and Jensen. At first sight we all noticed that it was showing the signs of a lack of money because everywhere you looked you saw things held together with spit and bailing wire.

Mr. Carpenter met us at the front gate and invited us in for coffee. It didn't take me long to size things up. Carpenter walked with a cane and his hair had gone from gray to white, and I figured him to be in his late sixties. I got the impression that he was not only ready to sell, but eager.

I introduced Jensen and Brooks as my advisors. Which was absolutely true since as far as the cattle business was concerned, I was a babe in the woods. I suppose I could have tried to bluff my way through and act like I knew what I was talking about but I'd seen men try that sort of a thing and end up looking like a fool. What was that old saying? Something about it's better to hold your tongue and let people think you're a lout, than to open up your mouth and remove all doubt. At least that was what I believed along with being honest with the man you were dealing with. Even if he was a horse thief.

Shorty walked up from the bunkhouse and Carpenter introduced him as his foreman. As it turned out, Carpenter wasn't only anxious to sell his cattle, but his whole outfit as well. Seems that his son was a big lawyer back in New york and he wanted his father to come back there and live with him and his family. Carpenter said he really wanted him there so that his son would have someone to back up the stories he was telling his friends about growing up in Texas. Stories some of them probably thought of as tall tales.

It wasn't long before we got down to talking about his

place and I found out that he was running about eleven hundred head of longhorns, fifteen horses, a chuck wagon, foodstuffs, and various other items I would need along the trail. He also had two other young cowhands and a cook who I figured would be needing a job. So while Shorty, Brooks, and I went out to look over the cattle and horses, Jensen went over to check out the wagon—and the men.

Carpenter had let it be known that his men would figure in the deal, so I figured it was best to know something about them before I obligated myself in any kind of a deal.

I'll say one thing for Carpenter—for a man who didn't have much money to work with, he sure knew how to raise cattle and horses on a shoestring. All of the cattle and horses were in in top-notch condition.

Back at the ranch, I took Brooks and Jensen aside for a quick conference. Brooks agreed with my opinion of the stock and Jensen sweetened the pot by telling me that the chuck wagon was in good shape and that there was enough foodstuffs and supplies available to keep our bellies filled for six or more months. As to the men, Jensen's first impression was good. The two cowhands were twins. Their names were Lester and Nester Cobb. They said they had been with Carpenter for about five years. Caleb figured them to be in their mid-twenties.

The cook was an old Mexican by the name of Juan Delgado. Said he had worked for Carpenter for over twenty years. And when Caleb had asked Nester Cobb how good a cook Juan was, he pointed to two riders headed in different directions. He said that they were both riders from different outfits who just happened to show up at suppertime. Happens at least twice a week that some cowhand manages to just drop by around suppertime. Cowboys riding the grubline have been known to travel a hundred miles out of their way to sit down in front of one of old Juan's meals.

Well, I have to say that I was pretty impressed with everything I had seen and been told. And I certainly intended to sample one of Juan's meals, no matter how the deal turned out. But for the moment I was mulling over a bunch of figures in my head as I leaned against a fence rail. I figured the cattle would cost about $2,200, the horses and mules to go somewhere around $450 and the wagon and supplies would come to about $300. Altogether I figured the cost to be $2,950.

That amount would bust me and not leave me enough to pay wages or even cover expenses that were bound to crop up on the way to Kansas. I'd be in a real bind until I sold my cattle. In other words I'd be in the same shape as almost every other cattleman in Texas at that time. The only difference would be that I wouldn't have a home ranch to come home to if everything went bust along the trail.

Shorty, Brooks, and Jensen all moseyed over to the bunkhouse to sample some of Juan's cooking, while Mr. Carpenter and I went into the house to do some serious bargaining. Figuring to do our business at the kitchen table, Carpenter pulled out a chair and indicated that I should do the same.

"I've done more business over this old table than I care to remember," he said. "Well, son, what do you think of my outfit?"

"Impressive," I answered.

"What do you figure it's all worth?" he asked, taking out a pipe.

Well, there it was, a chance for me to put my ideas about being honest with a man into practice. "If current prices are what I hear they are, I figure a low-ball figure for everything to be around three thousand dollars." And then I hastened to add, "But I can't pay that much."

Lighting his pipe, Carpenter leaned back in his chair and said, "I figure your guess is just about right. I'd also say that there are few men in Texas who could pay that much money for longhorns and run the risk of losing their shirts on a cattle drive. So I've got a little proposition for you." Crossing his legs, he continued, "Under certain conditions I'll let you have the herd, horses, wagon and supplies for two thousand dollars."

Leaning forward, I asked, "What are the conditions?"

"The first condition is that I get ten percent of what the cattle sell for when you get them to market. And if you keep any of the cattle to start your own ranch I expect to be paid ten percent of what they would have brought at market when you sold the rest of the herd. The second condition is that you guarantee employment for one year for each of my hands. That'll come to thirty a month each for the twins, forty a month for Shorty, and fifty a month for Delgado. Those, sir, are my conditions."

"What if something happens to the cattle?" I asked.

"Then you lose two thousand dollars and I lose one thousand dollars and neither one of us owe the other anything."

"What about the chuck wagon, remuda, and supplies?"

"They're yours no matter what the outcome."

I had to give that old man credit for being able to bargain, for if I made it to Kansas and sold the cattle at the going rate of twenty dollars a head, one thousand head would bring twenty thousand dollars and his ten percent of that would amount to two thousand dollars. Now I wasn't no great shakes when it came to working with numbers, but I did figure out that what he had done by charging me a thousand dollars less than what the outfit was worth and then tacking on the ten percent condition was, in effect, loaning me a thousand dollars for three months and charging me one hundred percent interest on it. Now *that* was slick.

And then, an idea occured to me and I said, "I would like to add one condition of my own to the deal."

"What is it?" asked Carpenter.

"That at any time I can deliver to you the sum of one thousand dollars before we reach Dodge City, I am free from any and all of the conditions you mentioned."

Well, now it was time for him to do some figuring so he took a scrap of paper from his shirt pocket and a stub of a pencil and started in on making some pretty serious-looking chicken scratches.

I don't know why I put that condition on the contract between me and Carpenter. It could have been that I was hoping that my good luck would follow me on up the trail and more money like the rewards I had recently collected would fall right in my lap. After all, a lot of strange things had been happening to me since I left Kentucky.

And then there was the possibility that I might just run onto a market for my beef before I ever got to Kansas. Then again, maybe I just wanted to beat this shrewd old man at his own game.

The only thing I knew for sure was that I was going to take the deal if Carpenter didn't accept my condition, for it gave me the means of paying all my hands three months wages in advance and gave me around five hundred dollars left over for expenses along the trail. All things considered it was just too good a deal to pass up.

It took a few minutes of studying and figuring, but eventually Carpenter decided that the possibility of my coming up with a thousand dollars in less than three months was too unlikely for him to have to worry about. So after a couple of minutes he reached across the table with his hand extended and said, "Done!"

Chapter Eleven
Cattleman

We were two weeks out of San Antonio and so far everything was going along fine. Shorty was acting as sort of a combination ramrod and schoolteacher who spent a good part of each day teaching me about cattle and how to run the outfit I owned.

Fortunately, I had always been a good pupil and could learn pretty much anything I set my mind to. And I had set my mind to learning how to be a cattleman. And Shorty believed in a man learning the business from the ground up so, even though I was the owner, I pulled my time in rotation. I rode night herd, singing to the cows, I ate a ton of trail dust, bringing up the drag, and every other dirty job a drover had to do on the trail. On this day I was riding point when a young cowpoke came riding up to me from the north.

"You bringing a herd up?" he asked.

Not being sure of his intentions, I let my hand rest near the grip of my pistol. I had already removed the thong when I saw him riding over the hill. "Yes," I answered.

"Where you headed?"

"Dodge City."

"How many head?"

"Around eleven hundred."

The stranger whistled low. "I can see you haven't heard about Hangtown," he said.

"Sure haven't. What about it? And where is it?"

"It's a gold-mining town south of Boulder, Colorado. Sprung up about a month ago when a couple of men made a big strike. Everybody and his dog is headed there."

"Well, friend, pardon me for askin' but ain't you sort of headed in the wrong direction?"

The cowboy grinned. "Not really, mister. I've got a pa who owns a big warehouse full of foodstuff in Dallas, and my uncle owns a freighting company. I plan on talking them into letting me take a bunch of those supplies on up to Hangtown." Relaxing in the saddle, he hooked his leg around the saddle horn and said, "You see, I've been in a few of these boomtowns and I've noticed that very few of the miners actually get rich. Most of the gold ends up in the pockets of the people who follow them, such as the merchants, gamblers, thieves, and the like. Why, I even heard about one feller who sold a bunch of cats to some lonely miners for ten dollars apiece."

We both just sat there for a couple of minutes, letting that thought sink in.

"If I was you, mister, I'd head that herd for Hangtown. There's no telling what a bunch of steak-hungry miners will pay for some Texas longhorns."

"We'll be noonin' pretty soon; want to join us? We got us a real good cook by the name of Juan Delgado."

"Juan? You mean you hired old Juan away from Frank Carpenter?" he asked, his mouth open in surprise.

"That's right."

I could see that he was trying to decide as to whether or

not he should take me up on my offer as he shifted nervously in his saddle. The greed in him was fighting a terrible battle with his stomach, but eventually his stomach won the battle and he followed me back to camp.

Everybody peppered him with questions at the chuck wagon, and he tried his best to answer them around mouthfuls of Juan's food. I have to say it was downright entertaining to watch him. He surely wanted to fork that old roan he was riding toward Dallas, but he was completely taken in by my cook's food.

I couldn't say that I blamed him for the last two weeks I had grown downright fond of the old Mexican's cookfire magic myself. He could use herbs and spices like no one I had ever seen before. I wondered how some of the fancy chow Frank Carpenter would be sampling in New York would compare to what Juan could throw together over some mesquite wood. I suspect that Juan would have come out the winner for I found out that Carpenter's son had been trying to talk old Juan into coming to New York for years as his personal chef. But Juan said he was born in the West and he figured to die there and not in some big city.

I was real happy that he felt that way because I wouldn't have bet against him if he said he could make boot leather tasty. He was that good at his job.

Finally, when the cowboy who had introduced himself as Jim Crane had his belly full, he pulled himself to his feet and mounted that roan. Walking over to our guest, I handed him a sack. "Thanks for the information, Mr. Crane," I said. "Juan made us up some bear sign last night and I thought you might find some use for a bit of it on your trip to Dallas."

You could see his mouth start in to watering when he

looked at that poke of bear sign. Thanking me for the sack and the lunch, he turned his horse and spurred it for Texas.

That night we all had a meeting around the campfire. In the end it was decided that since Hangtown and Dodge were at about the same number of miles from where we were now, that we might as well just continue on in the direction we had started. Shorty said that Dodge was already at an established railhead with buyers already waiting with ready cash. He said that Hangtown would be too much of a gamble. And then there was the problem of the number of unsavory characters such places attracted. He didn't think it too smart to be putting such a valuable prize in front of such men.

I had to agree with Shorty's opinion. I certainly didn't want to gamble on losing the herd. I'd already put enough on the line as it was. Besides, I could sell most of the herd in Dodge and then drive a small number on to Hangtown, if I figured I wanted to gamble on getting a higher price. And I was expecting a letter from Marie in Dodge. And it was there that I hoped to send her a telegram letting her know that the drive had been a success. And that she could expect me to return to Texas as fast as Bluegrass could carry me.

The next morning found me on the right flank of the herd trying to haze a particularly stubborn brindle steer out of a briar patch. I was swinging my rope when I felt a hard punch high up and on the left side of my chest. And about a half second later I heard a loud boom followed by several sharp cracks. Looking down, I could see my new store-bought light-blue shirt turning turning red in color right under my shoulder. Another blow struck my head and I slowly sank from my saddle and dropped to the ground.

I don't know how long I had been knocked out, but I did remember that I had been hit in the morning and that it was now dark. I also couldn't figure out why I was lying in mud. I hadn't been anywhere near water when the trouble started. Then I realized that the mud hadn't been made with water but with my blood. I'd lost a lot of blood and I knew that I needed help or at the very least, water, if I figured on surviving.

Trying to sit up, I immediately became dizzy and collapsed to the ground. My head throbbed and ached constantly and I could feel myself getting weaker by the second. And the thirst I had from the loss of blood was the worst I had ever felt. Lying there I forced myself to try and figure out where exactly I was at and what direction I should head in. Slowly my mind began working again and I remembered that there was a small stream about a mile to the south. And since none of my men had showed up, I figured that they must all be dead and that I had to get myself out of the mess I was in.

I figured that it would take me several hours of crawling to get back to that stream. Longer if I passed out along the way. As things turned out I had been overly optimistic concerning how long it would take me. I don't remember how long it took, but it certainly seemed more than a few hours. Then again, maybe time goes by more slowly when you try to cover ground from an ant's point of view.

When I finally got there I dropped my head into the water and drank deep and long until I began to choke and had to pull my head above the water to keep from drowning. I laid there gasping for air until I had recovered enough to stick my head back in the water and drink once again.

With my thirst finally satisfied, I crawled back from the water, curled myself into a ball, and fell into an exhausted sleep.

My eyes slowly opened to the first light of dawn. Sleep and the water had revived me to the point I could now sit up without passing out, and I began to take inventory. I'd been hit by the bullet of a heavy-caliber gun. Probably one of those buffalo rifles floating around the West. I'd taken the slug just below my left shoulder and while it had passed clean through, it had done plenty of damage and was restricting the use of my left arm. The second bullet had left a nasty-looking gash across my right temple. It looked bad when I saw it in my reflection from the stream but I knew that it would heal. But my shoulder wound needed serious attention real fast.

Continuing to take inventory, I was amazed to find that I still had my handgun and all my cash. Checking my pockets I also found some jerky and matches that I carried in case of emergencies.

Chewing on the jerky, I wondered what could have possibly happened. I'd been shot, but why? It couldn't have been to rob me for I still had my Colt and all my money. Even if they had only been after the herd, they could have stopped long enough to strip a dead man of his valuables. Well, that mystery was something I would try to solve later. Right then I needed to get to shelter and a doctor. And if memory served, the nearest town was Woodward, Oklahoma, and it was fifty miles away.

It would be a long hard walk. And the fact that I didn't have anything to carry water in, meant that I would have to be lucky enough to find water all along the way. Especially with my wound and the fact that I had already lost so much blood. Of course, I was lucky in the fact that I had taken to carrying matches and salve on my person so I was able to treat and bandage my wounds.

It was mid-morning so all I had to do was point my right arm towards the east and follow the direction my nose was pointing.

I was pretty sore and the sharp pain in my head had

settled down to a nice dull throb, but I still managed to make several miles before night fall. But my luck wasn't as good as I had hoped it would be and I had failed to find water and despite the terrible thirst that I felt, I knew that I had to get some food into me. Unfortunately, all I had was some dry and salty jerky. Still I managed to force some of it down and due to the exhaustion I managed to ignore my thirst and fall asleep.

The next morning I was wakened by a blast of warm air in my face. I had slept the sleep of the exhausted that night so I roused my self to wakefulnes very slowly and as I opened my eyes I became aware of a large nose in front of my face. It was Bluegrass. Surprised, I sat up with a start, and Bluegrass threw up his head and backed up a few feet. I sat there for several seconds wondering if I was dreaming. But when my eyes fell on the canteen on my saddle, my thirst overruled any doubt that my luck had returned and forced me to my feet. Grabbing the saddle horn to hold myself upright, I drank long and hard from the canteen.

With my thirst finally satisfied, I checked my horse over. I noticed a nasty bullet gash across his withers. Taking the salve from my pocket I smeared it on the wound. After that, I filled my hat with the rest of the water from the canteen and let Bluegrass drink. After that, I removed some jerky from my saddle bags to replenish the supply in my shirt pocket and eat on my way to town.

Tightening the cinch, I mounted and put the stallion into a gallop for Woodward. I had covered twenty of the thirty miles I had left to go when I spotted a familiar figure on the trail ahead. It was Shorty on foot and carrying a pack on his back.

He'd jacked a shell into his rifle when he heard me riding up behind him, but quickly lowered the rifle and smiled when he recognized who I was. "Thought we had lost you for sure, boss," he said as I rode up beside him.

Knowing that my horse could use some rest and that he would be carrying double for the rest of the trip to town, I dismounted and Shorty and I found us some scarce shade under which we could palaver.

Shorty laughed when I offered him some of the jerky I carried. "I think we can do better than that, boss," he said, opening up his pack.

Now I have seen some times that food looked awfully good to me, but out there on that grass I have to say what Shorty was packing looked like a feast. There were several sandwiches, coffee, and of all things there was a big can of peaches.

"I've been eating right well," Shorty said, as we put together a fire to boil coffee. "But I can see that a few days away from old Juan's grub has been pretty hard on you, so I'll just rustle up some of the chow he put together for me."

I was more than happy to let him do that as I put the coffee on the fire. And then I remembered my responsibility to my men and asked, "Where's the rest of the crew?"

"They're all back at the chuck wagon," he said, handing me a sandwich.

"What happened? I took a hit on the head and didn't even see who shot me," I said, just before biting into the sandwich.

Shorty poured a cup of coffee, handed it to me, and squatted back on his heels. "Two days ago, just before noon, about twenty men hit the herd. You were off on the right side and that's where they came from. I figure you was the first of our bunch to run into them. I heard a volley of shots and rode to the sound of the gunfire. I topped a hill and saw old Bluegrass there running flat out with a dozen men after him. I saw eight other men top a hill and come after me and every one of them had a gun out and was a shootin' at me. Figured you was a goner for sure. That's why we didn't come lookin' for you."

"Where were the others?" I asked.

"Brooks and Lester were riding left and right flank while Nester had the drag. Juan and Caleb were at the back of the herd greasing an axle on the wagon. Knowing that I couldn't win a gunfight against twenty men, I herded everybody back to the chuck wagon where we sort of forted up. I figured that was our only chance."

"You were right. If you had tried to take them on out in the open you would have been slaughtered," I said.

"Worked pretty well too. The only problem was that they really wanted that chuck wagon and the supplies. I figure that they wouldn't have fought us as long as they did if they didn't figure on using the wagon for their own drive."

Shorty filled his coffee cup again and took a bite of his sandwich. I took out my belt knife and opened up the can of peaches. "I still can't figure out why they didn't take the time to strip me of my guns and valuables," I said.

"That's easy enough to explain. They were in a big hurry to get to Hangtown. While we were forted up around the chuckwagon we managed to get lead into several of those bushwhackers. One of them was shot up so bad that he couldn't travel so his partners left him behind to die. After they left we went out and brought him back to camp and made him comfortable until he passed on. When he saw how we treated him compared to how the bunch he had teamed up with, he told the whole story."

Sipping my coffee, I propped myself up on my elbow to listen.

"Turns out they was just a bunch of ordinary folks who all got together back in Fort Smith, Arkansas, when they heard about the gold strike in Colorado. The bunch is mostly made up of drifters, cowhands, drunks, and the like. Leading the band is a man named Corby Nelson. He's supposed to be some crazy killer who escaped from Judge Parker's jail in Fort Smith. According to the man we took in, they been robbing folks all the way from Arkansas to here."

Taking another bite of his sandwich, Shorty continued, "When they stumbled on to us they just continued with their taking ways. It was Nelson who shot you with a fifty-caliber Spencer with one of those telescopic sights like they used during the war. You know the type that snipers used to pick off officers and such. And after he fired the first shot, they all opened up on you and after you fell out of your saddle, they all figured that you was dead. Some of them wanted to pick over your remains but Corby told them that they had bigger fish to fry than some down on his luck cowboy so they rode after the rest of the crew, and when they couldn't dislodge us from the wagon, they shot the mules pulling it and rode off with our cattle and horses for Hangtown. Although some of them did hang around for a while trying to catch that chestnut stallion of yours. But Bluegrass wasn't having any of that and wore them out leading their horses all over the country for most of a day."

"Did any of our crew get hurt?" I asked.

"Some of them got scratched up a bit, but nothing serious."

"You say they plan to drive them all the way to Hang-town?"

"Yep."

"That sure seems like an awful lot of work for a bunch of lazy thieves to be doing when they could sell them to places a lot closer," I commented.

"Sure does. And from what I saw of them they didn't appear to be the the type of men who had a whole lot of ambition. Then again, I've seen lazy men who would break their backs to carry gold out of a hole. I guess a little motivation goes a long way."

Sitting up, I said, "My guess is that they figure beef prices to be so high in Hangtown that they figure it's worth the trouble of driving all those steers all the way to Hangtown without the benefit of a chuck wagon and supplies. And they wouldn't be concerned about running the weight off the cattle since a bunch of meat-hungry miners wouldn't exactly be in a position to bargain. I figured them to drive the cattle as fast as possible.

"What about it, boss? What are we going to do?"

Usually I don't think very fast. I like to roll an idea around in my head for quite a while before I open up my mouth and start spouting off opinions. But this time it was different, the idea just popped into my head uninvited. "I don't know whether or not that bunch will make it all the way to Hangtown but wherever they end up, I plan on being there to take back what belongs to me. And I figure the way to start is to head on to Woodward, pick up some horses and mules, and take after the herd.

"Well," said Shorty, throwing the dregs of his coffee on the fire, "I reckon we better hit the trail."

Arriving in town just before dark, we quickly bought five of the best horses available and two mules. Shorty arranged for us to sleep in the barn so we could keep an eye on the stock since I had made myself a promise to be real cautious from now on. Part of my new caution caused me to rouse the town doctor out of his house that night to check on my wound. I sure didn't need to get out there on the prairie with a bad infection. I still didn't have the complete use of my left arm because of the bullet wound. I didn't need any more handicaps.

As it turned out I didn't have any reason to worry. The

doctor told me that the salve I had put on the wound had kept it from getting infected. So I thanked him and left some of the salve with him. He said he wanted to try to find out what was in it. All I could tell him about it was that it was given to me by an old riverman who'd gotten it from an Indian. But there was one thing for certain, the next time I saw John Rink, I was going to thank him for that salve.

Returning to the barn, I took the first watch as Shorty caught up on his sleep. The purchase of the horses and mules had shrunk my poke considerably and I intended that those blasted thieves reimburse me not only the two hundred dollars I had spent for the livestock but for my time and trouble. The way I felt about the situation that night, they'd be lucky if they got to keep their boots and pants after I got through collecting what I figured they owed me for the trouble they had caused. And the next day, we took up their trail.

Chapter Twelve
Two Herds

It was evening when we arrived at the chuck wagon. They'd sent Shorty out to get help and here he was bringing Lazarus back into camp.

Gathering them around the fire, I told them of my plan to chase down my stolen herd. I also told them that none of them had signed on for the kind of trouble I was planning on riding into and since I had already paid them their wages, they were free to leave with no hard feelings. As a matter of fact I told them that they would be plain fools to follow me. I said we'd be riding into a lion's den and not one of us was named Daniel.

Well, it was a credit to their courage that not a one of them quit on me. I couldn't say as much for their judgment. And some of them actually took offense to my even thinking that they might quit.

The next morning I figured I'd be the first one to roll out of my bed but old Juan had coffee and bacon on for me. Soon the rest of the crew joined us around the cook fire.

"Boss, I've been giving it some thought and I think we

ought to shake the brush around here some before we take out after that bunch of rustlers," said Shorty.

"Why's that?" I asked.

" 'Cause when that bunch came riding up on us they scattered the herd some. It wasn't a full-blown stampede, but I imagine we can shake more than a few head out of the brush. Maybe enough to put together a fair-size herd."

I thought about what he said and it made sense. "All right, let's make a gather. Start in close and work our way out. We will form them up behind the chuck wagon for now. Juan, you head the wagon in the direction that Nelson's gang is headed. We'll call a halt at noon and see how everything is going. I figure to keep up the gather as long as it pays."

Getting to my feet, I said, "Let's do it!"

Shorty was right—a large number of the cattle had spooked and most of them naturally gravitated toward each other after being used to each other having spent so much time together on the trail. But a few of them turned wild again in a short time and they were the ones that gave us nightmares and slowed the gather.

Two days later we had a little less than two hundred head back. On the third day we set out to catch what we were beginning to think of as the Nelson herd. Of course, following a herd of about nine hundred cows didn't require a whole lot of tracking skills. But what did slow us down was hazing the cattle that kept escaping from Nelson's inept cowboys out of the brush.

Another thing that kept interfering with the driving of the cattle was stopping to bury all the bodies we kept finding along the trail.

One day we ended up putting three bodies in the ground. The first one we found was lying facedown near a campfire. After turning him over we saw the cards under the body.

He'd been holding four aces and a queen. No doubt some-body thought that was too good a hand for him to have come by honestly, and had expressed his displeasure by putting two slugs from a .44 in the gambler's chest.

The second dead man we saw that day had died from a knife wound in the back and was lying in a ravine where someone had rolled him. The third one had been hanged. And I hated to think what kind of a crime he must have commited to rate being hanged by such a cut-throat bunch as we were trailing.

We'd been on the trail for three weeks and had gathered about five hundred steers. We'd also buried six outlaws and three settlers. It was plain to see that being a member of Nelson's gang wasn't good for one's health. And if you were a settler who happened to be in his path, you had better be well-armed or able to run fast. Because when his gang crossed paths with those who weren't well armed or inclined to run, he simply shot them and took whatever they had.

And when they ran up against a strong outfit, they traded with them, taking food, money or anything they figured they could sell in trade for the stolen cattle or horses they were driving toward Hangtown.

We ran into the first outfit that proved to be too tough for the Nelson gang on a Wednesday of our third week on the trail. Riding up into the ranch yard, I saw a tough look-ing old man striding over to greet me. He wore a Colt sidearm high up on his hip and carried a Greener double-barreled twelve-gauge shotgun at a ready position.

"Howdy," I said, reining up in front of him. I let my hands rest on my saddle horn where he could see them for on the way in I counted five rifles at various locations around the ranch being pointed at me and didn't want to give anybody a reason to start throwing lead in my direction.

Glancing past the shotgun toting old man, I noticed that the front door had been left ajar and through the crack a Winchester rifle was poking through, and whoever was holding it was wearing a calico dress. The lady of the house, no doubt.

"Howdy," replied the shotgun man. "What can I do for you?"

"My name's Matt Coltrane, and I'm driving a herd of cattle to Hangtown," I said, sitting my saddle as calmly as I could manage with five rifle muzzles pointed at me.

"Figured you was. Saw the herd, but what do you want with me?"

Shifting a bit more uneasily in the saddle, I said, "Right now we have about five hundred head of cattle. Three weeks ago we had over a eleven hundred head when a gang of rustlers hit us in Oklahoma. The reason I'm here is because you're the first settler I've found in their path who's still alive and I was wondering if you could tell me how many days I am behind them."

The old man visibly relaxed and let the shotgun barrels point to the ground at his side. "Light and come on in the house. I'll answer your question over a cup of coffee."

The inside of the house was plain with few fixins and homemade furniture. But the floor was swept and the rest of the house was spotless. The lady of the house was named Alice and her manners were a match for the grit she had shown holding that rifle on me a few minutes earlier. She poured the coffee for us at the kitchen table and brought out a big plate of biscuits and a jar of wild honey.

"For the biscuits or to sweeten your coffee," she said.

"Thanks, ma'am, I think I'll use it for both," I said, reaching over to spoon honey into my coffee, and then, breaking open one of the hot biscuits, I laid it on thick between the halves.

The man who had introduced himself as Noah Brewster said, "I'd sure like to see some sort of proof that you own that herd of cattle you're talking about."

I'd hung my hat on the chair next to me so I reached over and took the bill of sale Carpenter had made out to me and handed it over to Brewster. Taking some spectacles from a case his wife handed to him, Noah started reading the paper. When he was finished, he removed the glasses and put them back in the case. Handing me back the bill of sale, he said, "Seems I've got ten head of your cattle. That bunch sold them to me and made a bill of sale. Looks like I got took."

Working on my second biscuit and third cup of coffee, I chewed thoughtfully. "What'd you pay for 'em?" I asked.

"Twenty dollars a head."

"That's a fair price. Keep 'em. I'll collect from Nelson when I catch him."

Shaking hands on the deal, Brewster told me that Hangtown was about a week away from his ranch and that Nelson was about two days ahead of me.

When I left that ranch, Noah Brewster had a legitimate bill of sale for his ten head of cattle and I had a sack of apples he had given me to take back to camp. I had no doubt that Juan would be making up some fine apple pies and cobbler with those apples.

Before we made camp that night we picked up five more strays and counted the twenty-fifth steer we had found butchered. The fact that they didn't have a chuck wagon was playing hard on their stomachs and quickly shrinking my profits.

"What's next?" asked Shorty, as we all gathered around the campfire.

"We are a little less than two days away from Nelson's herd and I figure that puts them about three days out of Hangtown. How do you figure it, Shorty?"

Cradling his coffee cup, he said, "Sounds about right."

"I also figure that Nelson's gang had been whittled down to about eleven men," I said.

"Ten," interrupted Brooks. "I found another body to the south of here. He was shot in the back."

"Well, ten then," I said. "That's even better."

Taking a stick I squatted on my heels and started drawing a map in the dirt. Marking off where I figured Hangtown was along with our position and the location of the rustlers. Drawing a line that crossed in front of Nelson's path, I stood.

"Can the cattle make it over this route?" I asked, pointing to the line I'd drawn in the dirt.

Looking over the scratches I'd made, Shorty said, "Should be able to. That route is tougher with less grass and water but the cattle should be able to make it a lot faster. But I don't figure they can move fast enough to outrun a bunch of rustlers if you plan on stealing them and sneaking off in the night," he said smiling.

"You figuring on coming up on them in a couple of days?" asked Brooks.

"What then?" he asked.

"Haven't quite got that worked out yet. But I'd always figured on overtaking them at some point and they have been doing a good part of our work for us by driving most of the herd themselves. Of course, I wish they'd been better cowboys and then we wouldn't have had to spend so much time beating the brush picking up the strays they lost. Well, I reckon they're just better at stealing cows than they are at holding onto them."

"And you'll notice that they've been losing fewer head and slaughtering fewer steers lately. They're not doing that because they've become better cowhands all of a sudden. I think that they're tightening up because they can smell the money in the gold fields and they are beginning to look at those beeves as cash."

We all thought about that for a bit and then Shorty said, "I figure they got between three and four hundred head left."

Later that night, I had a conversation with Juan about something I would need if the plan I had put the finishing touches on in my mind was going to work. As it turned out Juan had the very thing I needed and would have it ready for me when I got back from the town of Fowler, Colorado, tomorrow night. I had an errand to run and if everything went as planned, the herd would be back in our hands in a couple of nights.

I set out at first light letting Bluegrass take the bit in his teeth. It was a pure pleasure for both the horse and myself to let him stretch out and run at full speed. I had thought about taking another horse to spell Bluegrass by switching back and forth on the ride between horses, but we didn't have another horse that could even begin to keep up with the the long-legged stallion.

I arrived in Fowler at noon. Stabling my horse, I flipped the man running the livery an extra two bits to see to it that Bluegrass was rubbed down and well taken care of while I was in town conducting my business. From there I walked to the saloon to purchase what I had come to town for and then, using the excuse that my horse could use the time to digest the extra bait of oats I had bought him, I had a big lunch at the only restaurant in town.

Carefully stuffing my purchases into the saddle bags, I mounted and started Bluegrass to where I figured the herd would be at nightfall. I had planned to take it easy on my way back, but my horse had been refreshed by his short rest and was feeling his oats. So what started out as a leisurely lope back to the herd, became a full-blown gallop.

As it turned out, Shorty had made better time than I had expected and I ended up several miles behind the herd. So it was completely dark when I stepped down from that big stallion at the camp.

Walking over to the chuck wagon, I spoke to Juan. "Just like we talked about last night," I said, handing him the well worn saddle bags.

Leaving Juan to his work, I turned to Shorty and the twins who had gathered around the fire. I asked them how the day had went. "Went fine," he said. "Of course, we didn't pick up any more strays, but we sure made good time. After we stopped for night camp, I rode on ahead for about an hour and I could see the dust that Nelson's herd is stirring up. If we get an early start and keep up the same pace we did today, I figure to catch them by mid-morning tomorrow."

Pouring my coffee, I squatted on my heels, and said, "We will pick up the pace and get ahead of them, taking the long way around. And day after tomorrow, we take our herd back and drive them on into Hangtown."

Shorty chuckled and headed for his bed roll. Looking back over his shoulder, he said, "If we plan on doing all that in a couple of days, I better clean and oil my weapons. Sure wouldn't want them rusting up on me when we tell Nelson that we want the herd back and for him to hand it over."

I had to smile. That Shorty had one heck of a sense of humor.

Thirty-six hours had passed and we were five miles ahead of Nelson's herd. We had built our campfire that night between two hills to hide it from prying eyes. I had already set my plan in motion, so I quickly ate and went to my bed roll where I planned to enjoy a long sleep because it wouldn't be my turn at night herding until in the morning.

The long night's sleep had refreshed me and my early morning duty had proved to be uneventful, so I came into camp early. After all, it wasn't going to be long before the cattle would be left completely unattended for a good part of the day. I would need every man in the outfit for my plan.

Riding in I expected to finally catch old Juan sleeping but I was disappointed Juan had coffee cooking the same as always. As a matter of fact I was beginning to wonder if Juan did sleep. Whenever I climbed into my bed roll at night he was always up fiddling with something or other. And no matter what time of night I rolled out of bed to ride night herd, I would see him smoking his pipe or doing one thing or another.

"Don't you ever sleep, Juan?" I asked, stepping down from my horse.

"Very little, señor," he said. "I always thought that life was too precious to sleep away half of it."

Nodding, I said, "Sounds like sound judgment."

He had turned and was starting in on making breakfast as I told him, "Bundle things up tight around the chuck wagon. I'm going to need you to help herd the cattle away from Nelson's camp this morning. You can herd cattle, can't you?" I asked as an afterthought.

Juan gave me a smile that showed many spaces between his teeth. "Señor, before my bones became so old I lived in the saddle as a vaquero. I am also very good with a pistola when it is needed."

"Then make sure you have your pistol with you because today you may well need it."

Just before dawn everyone began to stir from their blankets.

"Eat up boys, and make sure that you take something with you to eat while you're in the saddle. I don't plan on stopping today until the sun sets," I said, tightening the cinch on my saddle.

"I don't mean to be nosy, boss, but you haven't forgotten about those ten men with the Nelson gang, have you? You know that they ain't just going to sit back and let you run off with that herd they been pushing for the last month," said Shorty.

"That's exactly what I'm hoping for," I said.

"Boss, no disrespect intended, but did you fall off your horse and hit your head on a rock?"

Chuckling, I said, "Nope. Just mount up and take a short ride with me and I'll show you what I mean."

Shorty and the rest of the crew all walked to their horses and mounted. Shorty looked over his shoulder at me and said, "All right, Boss, let's ride into the lion's den."

Everyone was carrying a rifle across his saddle horn except for Juan who carried a double barreled shotgun and an ancient Colt stuffed into his trousers, as we topped the final rise with Nelson's camp below us. We had been hearing the cattle lowing for several minutes and everyone but Juan and me figured we'd be greeted by a hail of gunfire at any second.

The cows were milling about, ready to fall into the days routine of moving on. But nobody was riding herd and everyone in camp was rolled up in his blankets. Not one man was stirring. Shorty leaned forward in his saddle and whispered, "They sure get a late start in an outlaw camp."

"Let's see if we can wake them up," I said, kicking Bluegrass in the ribs.

We all rode into the camp at a gallop but none of Nelson's men offered to move. Dismounting, we fanned out, kicking and prodding the bed rolls. Still, nobody did much much more than grunt at the rude treatment they were getting. If it weren't for the snoring and the occasional twitching of a body every now and then, you would have sworn that they were all dead or pretty darn close to it.

Lester had ridden out to the cattle and was just coming back in when he said, "Three men down out among the cows."

"They alive?" asked Shorty.

"Mostly," replied Lester.

All eyes fell on me. "All right, boss, I give up. What caused this?"

"This did it," I said, holding up a whiskey bottle. "This and a little help from Juan over there. He made up a mixture of some herbs that slowly put them to sleep and should keep them that way for about a day."

"And when they wake up they will be very sick for another day," added Juan.

"Okay, that explains what knocked them out, but how is it that the whiskey got into their camp in the first place?" asked Shorty.

"Why, that was the easiest part," I said. "I just stuffed those bottles into an old set of saddle bags and dropped it on the trail in front of Nelson's men where I knew that one of them was bound to find it."

"How was it that you were sure that they would drink the whiskey?"

I couldn't keep from laughing at Shorty's question as I said, "A bunch like that turning down free whiskey? Aw, come on Shorty, you know better than that."

Smiling, Shorty said, "Yeah, I reckon so. Not drinkin' it would have sure gone against their nature."

"Yep," I said, "and because of that nature, we will have

plenty of time to drive our herd to Hangtown unmolested. And to make sure of that we're going to strip Nelson's gang of everything they have, and we're going to burn their clothes and boots. Let's see how well they rob and kill when they're put afoot and stripped naked. If they have any sense at all they'll head for Mexico where the weather is warmer."

It didn't take long to strip all of them of their valuables since most of them had next to nothing to begin with. The only man with a sizable poke was a man dressed like a gambler we took to be Corby Nelson. He wore a pearl-handled Smith & Wesson Schofield low on his hip and tied down. He also kept a derringer that was a match to the one I carried and an ivory-handled dagger in his boot. Confiscating all of the weapons, I found twelve hundred dollars in his wallet. I left him the wallet.

Looking over the rest of his men, I almost tripped over my own feet when I saw Tory Riley lying there. And close by there were his brothers, Rafe and Ollie. Taking out my tally book, I tore a page from it and scribbled a message for the Rileys, figuring that they would find somebody to read it to them.

Sticking the paper in Tory's hat band, I turned to Shorty. "How many cows they have left?" I asked.

"About three hundred," he answered.

"So these thieving idiots cost me three hundred head." Remembering that we left Texas with over eleven hundred head, and now I was down to eight hundred steers. Even back in Texas that was a loss of six hundred dollars. Up here with cattle going for at least twenty dollars a head, that loss grew to six thousand dollars. And that didn't even take into account the aggravation that Nelson's bunch had cost me.

"What are we going to do with this crew?" asked Shorty.

"Well, we sure can't guard ten men and push eight hundred head of cattle at the same time so I reckon about the only thing we can do is just leave them here afoot and naked and hope we run into some sheriff who feels like coming out here and arresting them," I said.

"We could hang 'em," suggested Shorty.

Not being sure as to whether or not he was joking, I said, "We'd have to wait around for them to wake up to do it."

Shorty laughed, turned his horse in the direction of the herd, and rode off. I thought that I had Nelson pretty well hemmed-in with the shape he was in and all, but I would find out later that a wagon train passing through would end up giving him a way out the fix I'd worked so hard to put him in. And if I had known the trouble he would cause me later on—I would have hanged him in his sleep.

We arrived on the outskirts of Hangtown two days later, and it was there that I figured my luck had packed its bags and headed back for Texas at an all out gallop.

Fifty heavily armed men came boiling out of that tarpaper shack of a town. And they were riding toward me at a determined pace. I was riding point in front of the cattle with my men far behind me. I didn't figure to have a chance. But I decided that I wasn't going to make the journey into the next world by my lonesome so I pulled my Winchester '73 from the scabbard and jacked a shell into the chamber. Sitting there in my saddle, I waited for one of them to open up the ball.

Chapter Thirteen
Hangtown

I had just thrown the Winchester to my shoulder, when I noticed that the men riding full out for me were waving and appeared to be grinning from ear to ear. If they were bandits they were the friendliest bunch I had ever heard of.

I let the hammer back down and shoved the rifle back into the scabbard. My initial fear that these men were bandits soon left me as they all stood around me, wanting to shake my hand and slap me on the back. Everybody was so excited that my hand was almost crushed several times and my back was bruised for several weeks after the greeting.

Everybody was trying to talk at once, firing questions so fast that I couldn't even come close to answering anybody. Finally, one man took charge and said, "Sure glad to see you, mister. Winter is just about on us and we need food. Things had gotten so bad that we were getting ready to shut down and head for Denver for to stay the winter." Several men nodded, confirming what he said. "How many head you got anyway?" asked the leader.

"Around eight hundred," I answered.

Cheers erupted from the crowd. "How much you asking?" inquired another man.

I sat my saddle for several seconds in silence. "I suppose we can talk about that in town, but I figure to sell them at some kind of auction. But I do have one condition on the sale. I think this condition is necessary in that when winter hits here full force all of you will be snowed in and you will need to make some sort of arrangement to see to it that everybody gets enough food to live on and no one man or group of men control all of the beef and start gouging everybody else. Human nature being what it is, I just wouldn't feel right to have driven all these beeves up from Texas just to let one man take advantage over another. However you want to work out a system to see that everything is on the up and up is fine with me."

There was a muted agreement among the men. It hadn't occurred to them that they might have to go through the winter being gouged by someone else who might have control of the food supply and they could see the wisdom of setting up a system that would guarantee a steady supply of food at a reasonable price.

"Where do you want the cattle?" I asked.

"There's a box canyon to the east of town that will work as a fine stock pen. Some of us will show your men where it's at," said the leader.

"Fine. By the way, my name's Matt Coltrane," I said, introducing myself and extending my hand.

"Lee Dillon," said the man who had quieted the crowd.

By nightfall the cattle were safely in the box canyon and my crew and I were sitting in a makeshift saloon being treated like kings. The bar of the place consisted of a couple of planks laid across two empty whiskey barrels. Jensen, who had seen several boomtowns before, said it never failed. You could be out of food, coffee, and everything else you might want in one of those towns, but you could always find two things no matter how hard times got . . . whiskey and bullets.

After several drinks had been bought in our honor, Lee Dillon and a group of what appeared to be the town's more affluent citizens joined us at our table.

"Well, Mr. Coltrane, we have come up with a plan I think you will find satisfactory. The town council, of which I am a member, has decided to offer you thirty dollars a head for your cows. And to make sure that everyone here in Hangtown will have enough food to take him through the winter, we intend to sell them to everyone at that same price through the entire season," said Dillon, as he leaned back in his chair and folded his hands across his stomach. "Is that satisfactory?"

Given that the going price was twenty dollars a head, I figured that a fifty percent higher price than we could have got in Kansas was more than fair, so I extended my hand and said, "Good enough."

I left my men behind to continue the celebration while I did some bookkeeping in a miner's shack that had been donated to me and my men for the night. Lighting the kerosene lantern on the table, I took out my tally book. According to Dillon, I had eight hundred and ten head. At thirty dollars a head that came to $24,300. That made Carpenter's ten percent cut come out to $2,430. The wages for the three months we had been on the trail had already been paid in advance. After paying Carpenter the only obligation I would have would be to guarantee nine more months of wages to Lester, Nester, Shorty, and Juan. I added that up to be $1,350. That brought my total liabilities up to $3,780.

I had made the decision to pay all of Carpenter's men in advance and to give Jensen and Brooks the same deal since anything could happen and I could end up broke at any moment, with my luck deserting me at any time. At least my crew would be paid no matter what happened. I also decided that since I'd sold all of my herd and had no cattle left to start a ranch with, it was a perfect time to go back to Texas for Marie. With her on my mind, I figured to give all of my hands the nine month's wages as a bonus and cut them loose to do what they pleased. I would decide what I was going to do after I talked it over with my soon to be wife.

So, figuring in Jensen and Brook's nine-month bonuses and the $2,000 I took from Nelson, I calculated my take from my first attempt at a cattle drive to be around $22,000. Not too bad for a boy from the hills of Eastern Kentucky.

I'd also given my men the outlaws' horses and guns along with what was left of our remuda as a part of their bonuses, and they were selling them to the miners. The way I figured it, every man in my crew was going to end up with over a thousand dollars in his pocket, which was more than enough for them to start their own ranch or business. The only thing I hadn't figured out was what I was going to do with the chuck wagon. I figured to decide about that tomorrow when I asked my men what they planned on doing. Blowing out the lamp, I took a bunk at the far wall of the cabin so I wouldn't be too disturbed by the late-night revelers who would be dragging in at all hours.

Everybody but the twins was able to get up the next morning. "Too much celebrating last night," said Shorty. "We were all lucky last night that everybody was in such a good mood, 'cause the way the whiskey was flowing if somebody had chosen to take offense at something that was said, we could have had one humdinger of a fight."

"Well, we still got some business to conduct, so try to rouse 'em if you can and pour some black coffee down their throats so they will know what's going on," I said.

It took about half an hour to roust the twins enough to get them to the point of where they could participate in our little meeting. I laid out the plan I had worked out last night and told them that my original plan about starting a ranch had been modified. I was headed back to Texas just as fast as Bluegrass could take me and they were free to follow or strike off on their own and try whatever they pleased. At any rate they had nine months' wages and the time to enjoy them.

"I haven't decided about where and when or even if I'm going to start a ranch, but if I do all of you are welcome to ride for me. I'd like to know what your plans are, if you have any, so that I can contact you and offer you jobs if I do start a ranch. I'm supposed to be paid at nine this morning and then that's when I'll pay you and head for Texas as soon as possible. If you plan on riding with me, be ready."

Caleb looked at Dell and Dell nodded. "Well, I don't suppose Dell and me have to keep you in suspense, Matt. We were planning to settle down on that ranch you had planned on starting, but now that we have enough money to start our own outfit, that is what we're going to do," said Jensen.

"Sounds like a good plan," I said, and turned to the twins.

"Mr. Coltrane, I guess Nester and me got us a case of the gold fever, and we'd kind of like to try our luck at mining. We figure to stay right here and file us a claim," said Lester.

"I can understand that," I said. "If I didn't have somebody waiting for me in Texas, I'd be awfully tempted to try my hand at finding some of that yellow metal myself."

Turning to Juan, I asked, "What about you, Juan? Got any plans?"

"As a matter of fact I do, Señor Matt. But it involves your chuck wagon and supplies. I would like to use them to open up a restaurant in the mining camp. But I cannot afford to pay the price that the goods would bring in this camp and expect to make a profit. I was wondering if we could make some sort of an arrangement for me to buy the wagon and supplies?"

I had to think for a few minutes because I knew that Juan was right. The wagon, mules, and supplies were probably worth as much as a thousand dollars at Hangtown prices. "Do you have any ideas, Juan?" I asked.

"No, señor, but I am sure that you will come up with a fair arrangement."

Thinking about how well I had been treated on my journey by Rink, and thinking of the deal I had made with Carpenter, I said, "How about after all of us take out a small grubstake from the supplies, you take the rest and pay me ten percent of your profits until the supplies are used up and then the wagon and mules become yours?"

"That is very generous, señor," he said.

"Done then," I said.

Finally, I turned to Shorty, and asked, "What about you, Mr. Costas? What are your plans?"

"My plan is to become a partner in your next business venture," he said.

"What business venture?" I asked. "I'm headed back for Texas to get married. I don't have any plans other than that."

"I remember all those nights we spent around the campfire on the trail up from Texas when we swapped stories and tall tales and sort of told each other our life's stories. You remember that, boss?"

"Yes," I answered, somewhat confused.

"Well, by my count, you left Kentucky a little over seven

months ago with seventy-five dollars in your pocket, and now here you are with over twenty thousand dollars and you didn't even set out to try and make money. With your kind of luck, I figure if we were to get snowed in up here, you'd end up owning this town inside of a month. I just want to get in on the gravy train when you decide you want to take off on some other project, that's all."

"That's an interesting theory you got dreamed up there, Shorty, but did you stop to think that it took the first seventeen years of my life to accumulate that seventy-five dollars I packed out of Kentucky?"

"You was just a kid wet behind the ears. Now, you're a full-grown cow man."

"Okay, Shorty. I think you're crazy, but the next time I feel the urge to risk my life and fortune on some crazy harebrained scheme to make money, you're in it also. We share the the profits—and the losses—all the way down the line," I said, extending my hand.

"Done!" said Shorty, clasping my hand and vigorously shaking it.

Chapter Fourteen
The Grizzly

The miners were as good as their words. That morning Shorty and I rode out of that town with over twenty-two thousand dollars in gold. The nearest town where I could wire that money to Argyle's bank in New Orleans was Pueblo, Colorado. So we headed south with Shorty astride a tall black stallion. It took some real convincing to persuade him to buy that big horse and leave his pinto with Juan to take care of, but I finally told him that with Indians running wild in the hills and a bandit behind every bush, I intended to put Bluegrass into a gallop everytime I saw a bush shake. And if he expected to stay anywhere near me, he'd have to have a mount that could at least keep me in sight.

I didn't have to tell him about what a tempting target we'd make when word got out about how much money we were carrying. I thought the safest thing to do with all that gold was to ride as fast as possible to a bank and safely lock it behind a steel vault. We also knew that the news of the cattle and us being paid in gold would spread like wildfire. And as proof of that we were only three days out when for the second time we spotted riders trying to overtake us. But those two stallions left them in their dust without even breathing hard. The pursuit had forced us higher into the mountains.

It wasn't that we hadn't expected for such a thing to happen since we had been told that no one who had tried to leave town with their gold had ever been heard of again. Dillon said that they planned to hire armed guards to come in and escort all of them out of there when they figured that they had a big enough shipment. They planned on doing so in the Spring. The miners also weren't surprised by what we told them about the Nelson gang. Several of the men had heard of him and a few had even had run-ins with him and his gang. We were assured that word would be passed on to the law about where they were at, and that if anybody showed around town barefoot, that they would be looked upon with a great deal of suspicion, and possibly hanged if they put up any kind of a fuss.

"I think that last bunch were Indians, and given where we are, I figure they were Sioux," said Shorty, as he rode up beside me and pulled over to the right to keep our horses from trying to bite each other. They were stallions and both meaner than snakes and full of vinegar.

"Then we better be extra careful about where we bed down tonight," I said, fighting the reins to keep Bluegrass from trying to bite Shorty's horse, or failing that, Shorty himself.

"I figure to make Pueblo by tomorrow night," I said.

"Yep, but I sure don't like the looks of those clouds," he said, pointing to the west. "They look like they're chock-full of snow and here it is we are in the middle of November."

"Why are you so worried about it?" I asked.

"Because winters in Colorado are bad enough, but winters this high up are killers. You don't want to get caught on one of these mountains if you can help it. People have been known to get snowed in up here and not be able to get out until spring, and those who didn't survive the weather didn't have to be buried, if you know what I mean."

I did know what he meant, and it made me shudder as I rode along, checking our back trail and wondering what we should do. "Didn't you say there was a cave pretty near here?" I asked.

"Just over that ridge," said Shorty, pointing to the southeast.

"Well, back home in Kentucky, when the weather starts to look the way it does now, it's a sure sign of a blizzard on its way. I guess we better find that cave and cut us enough firewood to last us for a week and settle in for a while."

"Sounds good to me, boss."

"By the way, Shorty, since we are now partners, there's no point in calling me boss anymore. Matt will do."

"Okay, Matt," said Shorty, as we kicked our horses and headed for the cave.

The cave went deep into the mountain with a small opening at the top surrounded by tree branches that would break up most of the smoke from a fire built below it and conceal our location. Unfortunately, we couldn't do anything about the smell of wood smoke and it was much too cold to try and go without a fire. We would just have to chance it. But other than the problem of the smoke we could build a good fire that no one would be able to see even at night and should remain fairly comfortable during the blizzard. We also had the added peace of mind of knowing that the snow would be destroying our tracks. During what was left of the day, we found several downed trees and were able to cut enough firewood to last for more than a week. That, along with the fact that we had packed in feed for the horses and grub for us, would allow us to hold up for quite a while without even having to leave the cave.

That first night of, what I began to think of as our imprisonment, we sat at the entrance of the cave drinking coffee and watching the snow fall. At first the flakes were small and few in number, but the size and number soon increased until your hand held out at arm's length disappeared in the wind-swept downpour. Finally the warm glow of the fire at the back of the cave lured us back to our bed rolls. And with horses near the entrance to give us a warning if anybody or anything approached during the night, we drifted off to sleep.

The next morning, Shorty was the first one up, piling wood on the dying embers of the fire. And seeing me start to stir, he said, "Glad you're awake, Matt. Why don't you start breakfast?"

Rolling out of my blankets, I grabbed the coffeepot and threw in some water and coffee grounds. "Salt pork and beans suit you?" I asked.

"You know me, Matt. I ain't all that particular. Whatever it is just make sure it ain't movin' and burn it a little on both sides," he said as he walked past me for the cave's entrance.

As I started to make breakfast, I thought about how much I was missing old Juan's cooking and I began to wonder about how good a cook Marie was. The more I thought about the situation the more I began to doubt my decision to leave Juan in Hangtown.

Later that morning, the snow stopped and the temperature went from what one might call a nip in the air to downright brutal. Shorty said that he figured that about two feet of snow had fallen last night and that howling wind we heard all through the night had formed some drifts that were a lot higher than that.

I wouldn't know how to even begin to try and explain to someone what it was like for two men who were used to working, or for that matter just moving around, to be trapped in a cold damp cramped cave for what they considered a long time. But I wouldn't have any trouble saying what the result was. You both got restless and on each other's nerves. That was the reason that Shorty and me decided to try a little hunting that afternoon. We didn't need the food and we didn't really expect to find any game. We both knew that game usually stayed in their dens when the weather turned bitter cold to conserve their energy. And while we were going hunting we weren't about to go around shooting off our rifles to let every renegade in the country know where we were on the mountain. We both planned on using silent weapons.

Shorty had a bow and arrows he had traded for back at the mining camp and I had a set similar to his that I had taken from those Kiowas back in Texas. And while neither of us figured to see much game, we also thought that a fresh rabbit or squirrel roasted over the fire on a spit would be a nice change from our regular fare and would give us a nice diversion from being couped up in that damp cave.

Shorty headed east and I headed west, with each of us agreeing to return to the cave an hour before dark. As I wasn't really expecting to find game because of the bitter cold, I was pleasantly surprised when I crossed the path of a snowshoe hare a mile away from the cave. Following the tracks, it didn't take me long to find the rabbit. Not that it didn't blend in well with the snow. For if it hadn't been for the tracks stopping fifty feet from where I stood, I would never have seen its white body. The thing that really gave it away was its tiny black eye that stood out like a sore thumb once I noticed the outline of the body.

Quickly nocking an arrow, I let it fly. The hare jumped into the air, landing on its side a couple of feet away—dead, with its blood staining the snow red.

Walking over to the rabbit, I picked it up and stuffed it into my game bag. Retrieving my arrow, I returned it to the quiver and started back on the trail to the cave.

The traveling was slow even though I was walking over the trail I had already broken and it was almost dark with me still a quarter of a mile away from the warmth of the cave. And while I was colder that day on the mountain than I had ever been in my life, what I heard next warmed me up considerable.

There was a loud crunching sound made by something very large running on the snow. I turned to study my back trail and focused on a very large blur moving very fast through a pine thicket behind me headed straight in my direction. Now, I was sort of stuck where I stood, having been pretty well frightened, but what I heard and saw next pretty well unstuck me.

There was a woof and then a bear broke out into the open. He stopped and stood on his hind legs. I took it to be at least eight feet tall and from the descriptions I had been hearing around campfires this had to be a grizzly, Old Ephram as the mountain men used to call him. That bear let out a roar that made every hair I had on my head and neck stand on end. And being that I was only armed with a bow and my handgun at the time, that roar gave me some real motivation to climb a tree. Looking around, I picked the largest and tallest one I could find near me and scrambled up it like a squirrel with its tail on fire. You would have thought that the thick sheepskin coat I bought back in Hangtown would have hampered my ability to climb that tree but it hadn't. It didn't slow me in the least as I climbed the ten feet to the top of that pine tree.

The bear stopped at the bottom of my tree and reared up pushing against the tree forcing it to sway back and forth as the bear's teeth snapped at my dangling feet. I was sorely tempted to unholster my gun and start blasting at that gaping maw but I still didn't want to bring attention to my location with the sound of gunfire.

Dropping back on all fours the grizzly stared back up at me with those little black piglike eyes in his dished out face and let out another of those blood-curdling roars. Taking the opportunity he gave me to steady myself, I locked my legs around the trunk of the tree and leaned outward to where I could notch an arrow. The movement spurred the grizzly to action and it once again reared to its full height to nip at my heels. The bear's weight against the tree caused it to shake so hard that I almost lost my grip and fell. Roaring once again, the bear turned its head and a blast of its hot fetid breath hit me in the face, causing me to gag.

Regaining my purchase on the tree, I drew back the bow string and loosed an arrow that flew straight into the bear's open mouth. The grizzly's jaw clamped down, snapping the shaft in two. Dropping to the ground the bear rolled on his back and started pawing at what was left of the offending arrow in his mouth. Quickly he became frustrated and worked himself up into a blinding rage.

Regaining his feet, his eyes locked onto the nearest object for him to take his rage out on. A pine tree a couple of feet from him got the nod and he rushed it, slamming it with all of his weight. So powerful was the charge that the tree uprooted and fell over. His fury unabated, the grizzly continued to slap the trunk with his massive paws, and despite the terrible pain in his mouth, he ripped out large chunks of wood with his teeth.

While what I was seeing was frightening enough in itself, what really scared me was the fact that the tree the bear had so easily knocked over was a much bigger one than I was now perched in.

Drawing my pistol I was determined to put some lead into that grizzly if he moved toward me again. I wasn't concerned about the noise anymore. Anyone stupid enough to want in on the fracas I was having with this bear was welcome.

It was then that providence took a hand in my fate in the form of a wide-eyed doe that busted through the brush and stood in the middle of the trail I had broken earlier. The deer and the bear saw each other at the same time. The doe reacted by swapping ends and running in the direction of the cave with the grizzly barreling after it.

I half slid, half fell down that pine tree and hurried after the bear. If Shorty was back at camp, I hoped he was alert and well armed.

I'd only covered about a hundred yards when I heard the gunfire coming from camp. But there was more than one gun firing. As a matter of fact it sounded as if a small war had broken out on the mountain. And from all of the roars and screams I was hearing I could tell that the bear was giving a pretty good account of himself in the battle.

In about half a minute, everything turned quiet and I tried to hurry along.

Slipping from tree to tree and using every bit of cover I could find, I made my way to the mouth of the cave.

Crouching low, I quietly moved toward the hairy hulk of the bear that was lying atop of a spread-eagled man dwarfed by the grizzly's immense size. With my Colt extended, I kicked the bear in the rump. When it didn't move I moved to the front and was relieved to find that the body under the bear wasn't Shorty. And there wasn't enough left of the man's face for anybody who didn't know him very well to identify him by. But there was something about him that I found to be vaguely familiar although I couldn't quite put my finger on it.

Checking where the battle had taken place, I turned up two more bodies. These I recognized as being part of Nelson's gang. Then I remembered that the man under the bear was also a member of Nelson's band of outlaws.

A scraping noise from inside of the cave alerted me and I spun around, gun to the front. The noise continued and I slipped to the back of the cave where I found a tied-and-gagged Shorty scraping his feet on the floor to get my attention.

Removing the gag and ropes binding my friend, I asked, "What happened?"

Rubbing his wrists to get the circulation going again, he said, "I'd been gone for about half an hour when Nelson and his bunch ambushed me. Of course they wanted to know where you were and where we were camped. I wouldn't tell them about you but they didn't have any problem finding the camp. All they had to do was to follow my tracks back to the cave."

Stopping to rub his jaw for a second, Shorty continued, "They worked me over pretty good trying to get me to tell them where you went. I figure they would have beaten me to death if one of them hadn't spotted your tracks. It was then that Nelson put two and two together and figured that you and me had been hunting and that you would be coming back to the cave sooner or later."

Looking Shorty over, I said, "Good thing they found

those tracks. When I first saw you, I thought the bear had gotten hold of you."

Shorty shuddered. "I heard the set-to that Nelson's gang had with that grizzly and saw part of it. I don't want nothin' to do with one of those things."

"How is it that those men outside got tangled up with the bear?"

"Nelson left those three behind to wait for you in ambush, and to kill me when they were finished."

Looking around the cave, I could see that our stallions, along with the three outlaws' horses, were in the cave. Walking over, I noticed that our rifles were still in their scabbards and although our saddle bags had been gone through, they were still there.

"They tried to take Bluegrass, but he bit and kicked so much that it stirred my black up and he joined in. Nelson was so mad that he told his men to shoot the blasted horse as soon as they got you. After that they sort of lost interest in the horses. Especially after they found your gold."

I was already interested in what Shorty was saying, but now he really had my attention. "How in the world did they find it? I thought I hid it real well," I asked, standing there in shock.

"You did. It was a pure accident. One of the men, named Rafe, was as nervous as a long-tailed cat in a room full of rocking chairs. He was jumping at every noise and when your horse started in to kicking and biting, he started to scramble up a wall where you had hidden some of the gold and knocked loose some of the rocks you had piled around it."

"Did you say Rafe?" I asked.

"Yep. And he knew you to. Him and who I took to be his brothers had a right lively dispute about you with Nelson. They didn't really want to be here when you got back. But Nelson forced them to stay. He wanted them to be the ones left behind to ambush you, but he couldn't force them that far. It seemed like they were more afraid of you than they were of him."

"We should have hanged that whole bunch when we had the chance," I said, with genuine regret. "And why didn't they all wait for me to get back to the cave?"

"Because Nelson wanted to beat the weather and get out of these mountains before they all got snowed in. The bunch the bear got were the only ones he could bully enough to make them stay behind."

Looking at Shorty's battered body, I asked, "You able to ride?"

"Might need some help getting on that tall horse of mine, but I can ride."

"Hold it, Matt," said Shorty. "Look outside."

Facing the entrance of the cave, I saw the snow. It was coming down fast and in large flakes. As I watched the snow fall, the wind began to pick up almost blowing the snow sideways.

Turning to my partner, I asked, "How long ago did they leave?"

Anticipating my next question, Shorty said, "They had enough time to get off the mountain if they rode hard, and when they left here three hours ago, they were riding hard."

Well, there it was. Ten thousand dollars of my gold was headed south in the hands of one of the most bloodthirsty cut-throats in the West. It was good fortune that they hadn't found the stash of gold I had hidden a few feet away from the one they found. Of the two it was the larger, since it also contained the money I owed Carpenter. That, at least, was a very bright spot in what was a disaster.

I had never wanted to go after something so bad as I did Nelson right then, but there I stood at the mouth of a cave, held captive by a blizzard. I could never remember a time in my short life when I felt so downright helpless.

Chapter Fifteen
Chasing Gold

It was two days before the blizzard stopped, and we estimated that two or more feet of fresh snow had fallen. Shorty said that we could have made better time if we had been on foot. That way we could have made snowshoes from willow branches and walked out a lot faster than our horses were going to be able to muscle their way through all of the piled up snow. But as soon as we hit open ground it would have been a different matter with us being on foot compared to how fast we could travel on horseback.

I soon found out how hard it was for a horse to break through snow that deep. Even horses as big as Bluegrass. It was also the first time I saw anything that could wear my horse down.

After about two miles of breaking trail I had to switch places with Shorty and let his black stallion take the lead. We soon discovered that two miles was pretty much the limit of either of the horses when it came to breaking trail. And it appeared that ten miles was the daily limit for both of the horses.

With the horses spent for the day, we were forced into

a lousy spot to make camp. We were out in the open with no cover and had to work really hard to collect firewood. Between being fully exposed in the wilderness and the howls of the wolves at night, I was really looking forward to seeing dawn when the horses would be rested enough to tackle another day of bucking the snow.

The only bright spot that night was the fact that we had brought the outlaws' horses out with us and were using them for pack horses and therefore had plenty of grub and supplies to use on the trip. Both for us and the horses. Banking the snow so it would act as a reflector for the fire and cutting pine boughs for beds that would keep us above the cold ground, we were able to enjoy a warm if not restful night on the mountain.

The next day at noon, we broke through the deep snow and found the trail to town. And a couple of hours later we rode into the growing town of Pueblo, Colorado. We both made sure to slip the thongs from the hammers of our six-guns as we rode down the main street. Our eyes swept the sidewalks and windows of the town looking for any sign of Nelson or his men. We had both become wiser and more cautious men from our experience on the mountain and we were well aware of the fact that we were outnumbered seven to two when it came to a showdown.

Finding the bank, we tied our horses to a hitch rail on a sidestreet close to the building. It didn't take me long to finish my business. Filling out a draft to be sent to Carpenter for the money I owed him I sent the bulk of the money to Argyle's bank in Louisiana. Given how many times I was running into people who seemed intent on separating me from whatever property I owned, whether it was cattle or gold, I felt safer knowing that most of what I owned was locked safe behind steel doors.

Walking back outside with Shorty, I asked him if he had

any money left after the Nelson gang stripped him of his poke.

"Got a twenty-dollar bill in my hat band," he said. "I call it my buryin' money."

Counting out five one-hundred-dollar bills, I handed them to him. "Before this is over one or both of us may need a doctor or lawyer. You can pay me back when we settle with Nelson," I said.

"Won't be as easy as the last time unless Nelson and his boys are considerate enough to drink themselves into a stupor," Shorty said, stuffing the bills into his pocket.

"Not likely," I said. "The teller in there said there's a sheriff's office down the street. Just to save trouble later on, what do you say to moseying on down there and having a little talk with him and sort of explaining how the wind's blowing?"

"Worth a try," said Shorty. "But I think Nelson's men might recognize our horses, and I'm sure that they will recognize the horses of the men they left behind. So I think it might be a good idea to stable the animals somewhere more private till our business is over."

"Good idea, go ahead and I'll talk to the sheriff."

I guessed the sheriff's age at about fifty. Of average height, he wore a black flat-crowned hat. I didn't know how good a sheriff he was, but he certainly looked the part.

Putting out his hand, he said, "I'm Sheriff Jeb Conners. What can I do for you?"

"My name's Matt Coltrane, and I'm here to report a robbery."

Motioning to a chair, he said, "Have a seat, Mr. Coltrane." Taking a seat in the chair behind his desk, he opened a drawer and took out some paper, an inkwell, and a pen. "Where did this robbery happen?" He asked.

"In the mountains about three days ago."

"What was taken?"

"Ten thousand dollars' worth of raw gold." If he was impressed with the amount, he didn't show it. "It was part of what I was paid for a herd of cattle I delivered to Hangtown," I added.

"Would you happen to know the name of the thief or thieves?"

"Some of them," I answered. "The leader of the gang is a man who goes by the name of Corby Nelson. The other three men whose names I know are Tory, Rafe, and Ollie Riley."

Finishing writing out his report, the sheriff reached inside one of the desk drawers and pulled out several wanted posters. Placing them side by side atop his desk, he asked, "Do you see any of the men who robbed you in this group?" He asked.

Turning them slightly, I identified them all as being part of the Nelson gang. I informed the sheriff about the dead ones and pointed out the ones Shorty and I were after.

Putting the posters into two neat stacks, the sheriff said, "Except for the Rileys, they're all in town and spending your money like it was going out of style."

"What happened to the Rileys?" I asked.

When Nelson and the rest got drunk their first night in town the Rileys stayed sober and headed south the first chance they got. Appears that they got tired of riding with Nelson."

I had mixed feelings about the Rileys. I was glad to get rid of them, but I wasn't real happy that they were headed in the same general direction that I was planning to go, but for right then I was wondering how it was that wanted men like those men traveling with Nelson were walking about so freely in town. I asked the sheriff, who said, "Well, to begin with, most outlaws ain't all that smart and most of them likes their comforts too much and that leads them to towns which leads them to the hangman's rope sooner or later. Besides, Nelson knows that most of my deputies are out of town right now and that I don't have enough deputies to take him without a lot of folks getting killed. But I got a real bad feeling that you plan on trying to take Nelson yourself instead of waiting for my men to get back. That about right?"

"Well, Sheriff, every day that Nelson's bunch is walking around free is costing me money and I'm chompin' at the bit to get even with that bunch of thieves."

Looking me in the eyes, and drumming his fingers on the desk, he asked, "How many men you got with you?"

"One," I answered, somewhat sheepishly.

"Well, you and him had better be real good with your pistols if you expect to live. And one other thing. My main job around here is to keep the citizens of this town safe, and I get paid well to do so. Make sure that no innocent citizens get hurt when you go after Nelson."

"Do my best, Sheriff," I said. "Could you tell me where they're staying?"

"Stable on Bleeker Street. Sign over it says the Royal. It's a pretty rough part of town, but you can usually find them in the saloon near the barn during the day. You can always find them there at night."

Tipping my hat to the sheriff, I said, "Thanks for the information."

"You're welcome. And I hope it don't get you killed, kid."

Walking into the saloon that night, Shorty and me had our hats pulled down low. We moved to the back and picked a table that gave us the best view of the bat-wing doors and everyone in the room.

"Recognize any of them?" I asked Shorty.

"The two over there at the table near the bar. The third one is in the corner watching his two friends play cards. But I don't see Nelson anywhere."

Seeing the large number of poker chips on the table, I noticed that Nelson's men had the smallest piles. "Looks like their luck has stayed bad," I said.

"But they don't seem to mind, do they? It's almost like they're not playing with their own money," he said, chuckling.

Shorty's sense of humor was getting on my nerves and I wanted to go over to that table and start knocking heads, but I figured that Nelson had the lion's share of my gold and I didn't want to tip my hand just yet by letting him know that we were in town. So I settled back to wait on him.

Five minutes later, an elderly gent ambled in and walked up to our table. Looking at me, he asked, "You Matt Coltrane?"

"Yes," I answered.

"Sheriff told me to give you this," he said, handing me a slip of paper.

Thanking him, I opened up the paper. It read: *Corby Nelson left town two hours ago. J. Conners.*

Crumpling the note, I said, "Nelson left town a couple of hours ago."

"What now?" asked Shorty.

"It's too dark to track him and the three men over there have robbed us twice. I don't figure on giving them any more chances to do that again."

"How are we going to handle it?"

I'd already been giving some thought as to how we were going to take those men, so I said, "You just sort of amble over to the one leaning against the wall in the corner. And when I brace the two playing cards at the table, you rap your pistol barrel right smartly against his head. Don't try to get the drop on him. They're all wanted for murder and I figure that they are all too desperate to give up without a fight. They will probably gamble against a drawn gun."

I stayed at the table as Shorty started to amble across the room toward the man leaning against the wall. That was when my plan came apart. Shorty's lack of height was something that people couldn't help but notice. And it was his lack of stature that garnered the leaner's attention that night. Pushing off the wall, he said, "Hey, it's that blasted sawed-off cowpuncher we left on the mountain. Get him, boys!"

Each one of the three reached for iron at the same time. Shorty had been caught out in the open with his hand no where near his gun.

Yelling for Shorty to take cover, I went for my Colt. With their intended target diving under the table, all eyes turned toward me as they began to swing their weapons in my direction. But I got my .44 unholstered and leveled first. The leaner was the first to go down with a hole in his chest just above his heart. The gunman sitting nearest the leaner had stood up and was leveling his weapon at me and was earing back the hammer. I snapped off a hurried shot and his gun and gun hand were ruined forever.

Letting my right knee buckle, I dropped to the right just as a .45 slug scratched my left cheek and notched my ear. Dropping further to the right, I cocked the hammer on my gun and brought it to bear on my attacker. When the front sight of my pistol lined up on my target, I saw the muzzle of his .45 blossom a bright orange color and I felt the 255 grain whip by my temple. A split second later, my .44 bucked in my hand and he went down with a hole between his eyes.

Pulling myself up on the table I sank back into my chair.

Soon everyone was coming out from under tables or whatever cover they had taken when the fight started. At least the sheriff should be happy, I thought, because none of the townsfolk got shot in the gunfight. Shorty had risen from under the table and had pulled his weapon. Nodding to him, I began ejecting the spent shells from my Colt and started jamming fresh ones back into the chambers.

As I was doing that, the man whose gunhand I had ruined was reaching for his partner's pistol with his good hand. Shorty rushed over to where he was and ruined his other hand with the heel of his boot and rapped him alongside of his head with the barrel of his pistol.

It wasn't very long after that that the sheriff showed up with a double-barreled shotgun and deputy in tow. Looking things over, he said, "Well, Coltrane, looks like I can get rid of some wanted posters. Any citizens hurt?"

There was a subdued buzz in the room as some of the more drunken patrons started checking themselves for bullet holes.

"Reckon not, Sheriff," I said.

"Good," said the sheriff. And then turning to his deputy, he said, "Luke, find the undertaker and tell him that he's got some business courtesy of Mr. Coltrane here." Then motioning for me to join him, he said, "Coltrane, you and your partner can go through their pockets. Whatever you find is probably yours anyway. And what isn't was probably paid for with the gold they stole from you. Just leave ten dollars for each man you killed to cover burying expenses—not that you're required to pay for their funerals, but I am fining you for discharging a firearm within the city limits," he said, chuckling as he helped his deputy and some volunteers drag the bodies out the door.

Later, as we were checking out of the hotel, the clerk told me that there was letter for me. "I'm sorry, Mr. Coltrane, but I've been training a new clerk, and since this letter has been here for some time, he didn't know to give it to you," said the clerk.

"That's all right," I said. "But I would like to know how this letter found me here since I didn't even know I was going to be staying here until yesterday."

"That's not hard to explain," said the clerk. "We're the only hotel in town, and the man who runs the post office figures that anybody traveling through town will end up here sooner or later. He keeps a record of the letters he leaves over here in case somebody is expecting a letter and stops by the post office. but he figures that this is the best place to leave the mail for strangers, especially if they aren't looking for any mail."

Thinking about it for a few seconds, I said, "Makes sense."

Turning the letter over in my hand, I could see that it was from Milt Warren. Taking it over to a couch in the lobby of the hotel, I opened it up. It read:

Matt:

Marie's relatives in New Orleans tried to kill her here in Texas. She was afraid for us so she ran off and didn't tell us where she was going. I fear that she is in great danger.

Milt Warren.

Handing the letter to Shorty, I sank down into that leather couch, once again in despair. What was I supposed to do now?

Reading the letter, Shorty handed it back to me, and asked, "The girl you were planning on marrying?"

"Yes," I answered mournfully.

We both just sat there for several minutes, deep in our own thoughts, when I remembered the business card I always carried. Fishing around in my pockets, I finally came up with the card John Rink had given me back in New Orleans. It had a New York address. Jumping to my feet, I said, "Come on, Shorty, we're going to send a telegram all the way to New York."

It took a short time to find the telegraph office, but it took a bit longer for me and Shorty to compose the message I wanted to send since neither of us had ever sent a telegram before.

Finally, we put together one that read:

Marie in danger from her family. Has fled for parts unknown. Need help finding her. Will be in Amarillo, Texas, for reply.

Matt Coltrane

Since I had no idea which way Marie had run, I thought I might as well chase after Nelson, until I found out where Marie was. So we tore out of Pueblo that morning with my body chasing Nelson, but with my mind on Marie.

Nelson had a jump on us and we had found out that he had bought the fastest horse available in Pueblo and had headed south. A smart man would have headed for the wilderness and lost himself. But Nelson was a man who loved towns with their saloons and gambling. So I figured to stop in every town we came to.

The first town we arrived in was Trinidad, Colorado. We got there at night and headed straight for the stable. We knew that Nelson was riding a big bay gelding.

A quick check of the barn didn't turn up the horse, but we knew that he figured we could be on his trail and he would have taken steps to hide his mount from prying eyes.

Failing at our first attempt at finding Nelson, I suggested that we grab a quick supper and set up a watch in the nearest saloon. I kept our mounts out of sight while Shorty made some discreet inquiries about where the best place was in town if you wanted to hide your horse.

An hour later Shorty returned. "Find out anything?" I asked.

"There's a hitching rail in the red light district of town. Everybody on the run ties his horse to it if he doesn't plan on being in town for very long."

"Well, let's go over there and see if there's a big bay tied to that hitch rail," I said, mounting Bluegrass.

Riding in the direction Shorty had been told we halted at the hitch rail, dismounted and tied our horses next to a big bay gelding. We both wanted to go through those batwing doors with our guns drawn, but we held back.

He already knows what you look like, so find yourself a wall to lean against until you can walk in without being noticed," I said.

"What's to keep him from noticing you?" asked Shorty.

"He's never seen me," I answered.

"What?"

"That's right, If you'll remember, he shot me with a rifle at a long distance; he was knocked out when we took the herd back, and I was out hunting when he stole the gold. So he's never seen me up close."

"Durn, if you ain't right," said Shorty.

"So you just sort of hang around out here while I go inside and try to locate him," I said, loosening my pistol in its holster.

Shorty did what I asked, taking up a position outside the doors while I strolled on in. The light in the saloon was dim but I didn't have any problem spotting Nelson. He had shown a definite preference for wearing black coats, white shirts, and those little string ties that gamblers appeared to be so fond of. He also had grown a moustache since the last time I saw him, and it appeared to be turning gray. I made him to be around forty years old. And the very fact that he had managed to stay alive as long as he had with his taking ways being as bad as they were, spoke highly of his ability to survive in the dog-eat-dog kind of circles he traveled in. And I knew I should be cautious of that .44 Smith & Wesson stuck into his pants.

Soon a spot at the table opened up and I took the seat. It wasn't that I wanted to gamble, but I did want to see if Nelson had recruited any more men since leaving Pueblo. I didn't want to try to brace him and have one of his men shoot me in the back.

"Straight poker, nothing wild. One-dollar ante and unlimited raises," said Nelson.

"Fine with me," I said, and bought fifty dollars' worth of chips.

Sitting in on the game for several minutes, I didn't see anyone who seemed to be friendly with Nelson. But I did see that my backup in the form of Shorty arrive. He came in with a group of men so he wouldn't bring any attention to himself and took up a position in the back of the room.

The deck had made the rounds among the players sitting at the table and Nelson was once again the dealer. He was good. But my eyes were young and quick. An uncle had taken over my education when it came to teaching the ways of gambling since my pa had never held with the practice, and he had taught me how to spot the tricks used by crooked gamblers. And I could see that Nelson had also had an instructor to teach him the ways of some of those Mississippi riverboat gamblers. And it appeared that he was fond of using all of the tricks, from stacking the deck to dealing off the bottom.

I guess I wasn't the only one who noticed that every time it was his turn to handle the cards, he seemed to end up winning. Of course these were just cowhands and they hadn't enough experience or drunk enough liquor to begin to call Nelson the cheat that he was.

As the game progressed I began to see that Nelson didn't appear to have hired on any new men, for no one seemed likely to come to his aid if I braced him. As a matter of fact, the men sitting around the table with me looked more like they would have liked to carve up his liver with a real dull knife.

"How many?" asked Nelson, holding the deck in one hand.

"One," I answered. "And this time I'd like to have it dealt from the top of the deck for a change."

Now, if I manage to live to a ripe old age, I'll never stop being amazed at how fast a noisy saloon can get dead quiet when somebody utters a few little words like I just did. Not to mention how fast chairs can be moved out of the way between two men who are getting ready to start throwing lead at each other.

"What are you trying to say, kid?" asked Nelson.

Pushing back my chair, I stood up facing him and said, "What I'm saying, Corby Nelson, is that as well as being a rustler, thief, and murderer, you're also a card cheat."

I could see the calm he showed to the world leave his face and could see some tiny beads of sweat start to form on his upper lip. "Who are you, boy?" he asked, keeping his hands on the table where I could see that he wasn't going for his gun.

"Matt Coltrane," I answered.

He gave an involuntary jerk and the cheroot he was smoking dropped from his mouth. I could see that he was scared, but he also had the look of a cornered cougar about him, and all of my instincts were screaming that I was at the very brink of death. The next few seconds passed by in a blur. While my hand seemed to move in slow motion, he was quicker and before I knew it, a derringer shot out from his sleeve and into his left hand. Almost immediately I could see the barrel smoking and feel the slug slamming into the left side of my chest. I had fallen but was still clawing for the Colt at my side when I saw Nelson reaching for the Smith & Wesson stuck down in his waistband. I had known that to try to take on a killer like Nelson in a gunfight wasn't the smartest thing to do, but I was young. I was angry, and I had faith in my skill with the Colt that I wore, but it was my lack of experience that was about to put the final nail in my coffin that night as I saw him pull the weapon, level it at my head, pause, and say, "You sure did have the Riley boys buffaloed, Coltrane, but I told them that you wasn't nothing but some snot-nosed kid who just got lucky and that one day your luck would run out. Well, kid, looks like today's that day."

I heard the shot and then everything went black.

Chapter Sixteen
Showdown

My eyes slowly focused on a bald fifty-year-old man wearing a black vest and one of those listening devices like old Doc Walters used back home in Kentucky. I tried to speak but my voice didn't want to cooperate so all that came out was a scratchy croak.

The doctor immediately put his hand on my forehead and looked into my eyes. "Well, I can see that you've decided to rejoin the living," he said, as he checked me over.

I tried to speak again and managed to get out, "Where am I?"

Removing the earpieces of the stethescope, he said, "Take it easy Mr. Coltrane. I'll try to anticipate your questions so you won't have to try and talk. First off, I'm Doctor James Benson and you are in a room above my office in Trinidad, Colorado. You were shot two weeks ago by a man with a .41 caliber derringer. The bullet went deep into your chest, but by some miracle it didn't hit anything vital. But it was still too close to your heart for me to try and dig out."

Tiring, the doctor pulled up a chair and sat down as he

continued his story. "Fortunately for you, there happened to be a young surgeon from back East who was visiting his folks. I tell you I've never seen such skilled hands in my life. He dug out that slug in nothing flat. But even with him getting that bullet out of you without you dying, it was still pretty iffy as to whether or not you were going to survive. For my part I was ready to write you off, but your friend told me that you was one lucky hombre and he'd take all bets against you not pulling through."

"Where . . ." I croaked.

"He's right outside the door," answered the doctor. "I'll get him," he said, rising from the chair and quietly leaving the room.

The door slowly opened and Shorty walked in twisting the brim of his hat in his hand. "How you doin', Matt?" he asked.

"Fine," I squeaked.

"Yeah, you look real good," he said, smiling.

Pulling the doctor's chair up by my bed, he said, "Nelson got two shots off and was just about to shoot you again when I plugged him."

Closing my eyes, I remembered the shot. I had thought it was Nelson finishing me off but it had been Shorty doing it for him instead.

"By the way, Matt, there was a two-thousand-dollar bounty on Nelson. I also found five thousand dollars' worth of your gold on him. I figure that with the reward and all, that you are right back to where you were before they robbed us. At least you are moneywise."

He was right about that for I was ending up with as many holes in me as an pair of my old pants. "The doctor said I've been out for two weeks. There may be news about Marie in Amarillo," I said, trying to raise myself up right in the bed, but falling back instead.

"Take it easy, Matt," Shorty said. "I knew that you would want to know about her, so as soon as I saw that you were going to pull through, I rode to Amarillo to see if there was a message about her. Marie has been found and is safe. And there was more than a telegram waiting for me when I got there. There was one of those Pinkerton detectives. He told me that he had been hired by John Rink. And as a matter of fact, Rink had hired several Pinkertons to find and protect your fiancée."

"Where's the Pinkerton at now?" I asked.

"He rode back here with me. He's supposed to report to Rink as soon as you get back on your feet."

There was a knock at the door and Shorty went to answer it, letting a tall, dangerous-looking man wearing city clothes, enter the room. The stranger stuck out his hand and said, "My name is Frank Bowler, and I work for the Pinkerton Agency."

Taking the offered hand, I shook it with as much vigor as I could muster at the time. I motioned for him to take the chair Shorty had been occupying.

Removing his hat, he sat down and launched into his story. "When contacted by Mr. Rink, the agency began an investigation into Miss Laborteaux's background in an effort to find her. Through that investigation, we came across the name of a lawyer in New Orleans by the name of Phillip Lawson who was retained by Miss Laborteaux to do some legal work for her. Specifically, to look into her rights as an heir to her grandfather's silver mine in Nevada. As it turns out, she is entitled to a full one third share in all of the assets of her grandfather's estate. It comes to very large sum."

Reaching into his pocket, the agent took out a cigar, bit off the end and lit it. He continued, "There also seems to be a question concerning what has happened to some of the other people who were entitled to share in the inheritance. Seems that either they have all turned up dead or disappeared. And it appears that with Marie's aunt and uncle being the only other survivors of the family, more than a little suspicion has been generated about their guilt in the matter. At any rate, enough evidence has been found to freeze all of their assets until a trial can be held."

"Where did you find Marie?" I asked.

"Working in a restaurant in Kansas City. It seems that her aunt and uncle had sent some people to kill her so we sent three body guards to watch her night and day. We had planned on keeping her in Kansas until the trial but when she heard about you getting shot, she decided to come to Trinidad to be with you."

"Did all of the guards stay with her when she left Kansas?" I asked.

"Certainly. As a matter of fact, Mr. Rink ordered that the number of Pinkertons be doubled for the trip." Removing the cigar from his mouth, he said, "As for me, I was told to ride here and bring you up to date, supervise the setting up of a security detail when Miss Laborteaux arrives, and send back a complete report of the entire operation."

Rising from the chair, he said, "And I intend to get to the paper work right now. If you gentlemen will excuse me, I have to get back to my room and get to work on that report." Tipping the brim of his hat, he turned and left the room.

As the Pinkerton left, Shorty once again took a seat in the chair. "Looks like things are shaping up real fine," he said.

Struggling, I managed to bring myself up on one elbow and said, "Not quite. Don't forget there's still two people out there who still want Marie dead."

The next three days I rarely was able to get out of bed, and when I could it was only for very short periods of time. On the fourth day I was able to go for a short walk, having to stop often to rest. By the fifth day, I was able to strap on my handgun and take all of my meals at the cafe down the street. On the sixth day I was hobbling all over town with the aid of a cane Shorty had given me.

That night Shorty and I were sitting in the saloon drinking beers. Shorty was engrossed in a fascinating game of solitaire, while I was occupying my time by watching the swinging doors at the entrance of the saloon. I was particularly interested in the faces of people that I hadn't seen around town before. A couple of strangers in particular had peaked my interest. I couldn't quite place them until I noticed the one wearing a bowler hat—the type that cowboys were so fond of shooting off the heads of dudes. It was then that I remembered where I had seen them before: they were the men posing as lawmen who tried to take Marie off the wagon train. Looking closer at the hat I could see a large hole in the crown. I was beginning to wonder why they hadn't recognized me but then I remembered that I had been in the background when Milt had his run-in with them.

Walking over to the far end of the saloon they took a table where they would have a good view of the bat-wing doors. A few minutes later a man walked through those doors who almost made me choke on the beer I was drinking—it was Marie's uncle. Walking over to the man with the bowler and his partner, he took a seat at their table. From the way they were looking around the room it was obvious that they were trying to locate someone.

Kicking Shorty under the table, I said, "Marie's uncle just walked in. He's over at the table with the other two men dressed in black."

Shorty casually glanced in the direction I had indicated

and said, "The two with him have been in town for three days, and they've been asking a lot of questions."

We watched them as they roamed around the room. They were obviously fishing for information. And it wasn't long before Shorty and I knew who they were looking for when we saw a cowboy pointing me out and the man wearing the bowler hat look across the room directly at me. The three of them quickly came together and started casting furtive looks in my direction. And then they all got up and left together.

Shorty, who witnessed their antics, said, "You don't suppose that they might have heard about the gunfight you had and were just curious about what you looked like, do you?"

Smiling, I asked, "Do you?"

The next day, flanked by four outriding Pinkertons, Marie arrived in Trinidad on the stage.

Running up the sidewalk after seeing me, she threw her arms around me with such force it caused me to wince in pain.

As she stepped back, she could see the grimace on my face. "Oh, I'm so sorry, I forgot that you were injured. Does it hurt much?" she asked.

Holding her at arm's length, I said, "Only when pretty girls squeeze me too hard," I answered.

Looking up at me, smiling, she said, "Has that been happening a lot around here? Maybe I should find someone who isn't so apt to end up getting himself shot full of holes so I won't have to worry about such things."

We both stared at each other for a couple of seconds before we both broke out laughing. Taking her arm, I escorted her to the hotel, preceded and followed by a parade of Pinkertons.

That night Marie, Shorty, I, and Frank Bowler had a late

supper at the finest eatery that Trinidad could provide. But it wasn't just four people getting together to enjoy a fine meal. It was also a strategy session. And Bowler was in charge of it. "Miss Laborteaux," he began, "your attorney suggests that you return to Texas as soon as possible. He has done all of the legal work to secure your inheritance and he feels that you should be back there to take the reins of your family's fortune as fast as you can."

Marie sipped the wine in front of her, and said, "I plan on letting my husband handle those matters, Mr. Bowler."

"As you wish, Miss. Mr. Coltrane has informed me that your uncle is in town along with a couple of other toughs. So please don't go anywhere alone."

Touching my arm, she said, "I have no intention of going anywhere alone, sir."

"Very good," he said. "And now, if you will excuse me, I have to work out a schedule for your guards tonight."

Shorty finished his supper and excused himself, leaving me and Marie alone to discuss our future plans and to catch up on what happened to us since we last talked in New Orleans.

The evening was pleasant and I felt like I was walking on air that night as I escorted her back to the hotel. But the danger that Marie was facing put a damper on my good mood. And every time that I momentarily could put that out of my mind, I would notice Shorty and the Pinkertons following at a discrete distance.

Bowler had taken over all of the rooms on the second floor, with Pinkerton agents in every room not occupied by Marie, Shorty, or myself.

There was also an agent stationed outside of Marie's door and one stationed in the lobby. It was their job to stay awake for the entire night.

It all looked very efficient and foolproof. But I still didn't plan on trusting to luck. So, asking Marie to wait at her door, I took Shorty aside, and said, "I plan on sticking some bundles under the blanket on my bed and sleeping on the floor and I advise you to do the same."

"Sounds like a good idea," he said, opening his door. "See you in the morning."

Opening Marie's door, I told the guard that I would be spending the night in her room. Once inside, Marie said, "Why Mr. Coltrane, I had no idea that you were so bold. I can just imagine what Mrs. Warren would have to say about such improprieties." Standing there with her hands on her hips, I could see that she was having a hard time keeping from laughing as she feigned being shocked.

Walking over to the bed, I stripped the blanket and sheets from the bed and covered a pillow with them to give the impression that some one was sleeping under them.

Pointing to a chair, I said, "I'll be sleeping in that and you'll be sleeping in the corner where I piled most of the bedding."

"You expecting trouble?" She asked.

"You notice how frail these doors are? One good kick and they'll fold up like a house of cards."

When I was finished, I took her over to the spot I had picked for her. Kissing her, I said, "Good night, Marie."

She gave me a puzzled look.

Knowing that she was wondering why I would choose to sleep so far away from her, I said, "I can't afford to be distracted tonight. And I find just being in the same room with you to be too distracting as it is."

Smiling, she set about making up her bed. I removed my coat and took the other pistol I had stuck behind my back and moved it to the front of my waistband. It was a nickel-plated Colt of the same caliber as my other pistol. The only differences being that it had a 4 ¾ inch barrel and was equipped with stag grips. Shorty had taken it from the leaner I had shot in Pueblo. He said I might like to have a spare pistol. And on this night I was more than a little happy that I had accepted the weapon.

Settling down in my chair, I was about to pull the hat down over my eyes when I noticed that Marie had laid the ivory handled derringer I had given her back in New Orleans by her side.

It was very close to daybreak. The time when most people are enjoying the last of a good night's sleep. And everyone in the hotel was asleep that morning, except for the guard outside Marie's door and the one in the hotel lobby. They were dead—poisoned by the coffee they drank to help them stay awake.

A boot struck Marie's door, and as I had predicted, it splintered. The two men who had been with Marie's uncle in the saloon, rushed into the room and emptied double-barreled shotguns into the pillow I had covered with a blanket. The room filled up instantly with black powder smoke and goose feathers from the pillow.

Pulling the stag handled Colt, I raked the hammer as fast as I could, pouring bullets into the would-be murderers' bodies. They had dropped the shotguns and were clawing for their pistols as my bullets plowed into them and they fell onto what was left of the door.

Sticking the empty .44 back into my waist band, I drew the holstered revolver. Glancing to my right to check on Marie, I could see that she had opened the barrels of her derringer and was stuffing shells into the chambers. Thinking of the compliment that Rink had paid me, I couldn't help but think that Marie would also do to ride the river with. Seeing that I was looking at her, she said, "I'm fine."

Running to the door, I stepped into the hallway and saw the Pinkerton guard slumped over in his chair. The hallway was filled with smoke and it was hard to see very far, but I did catch a movement out of the corner of my eye in time to duck back into the room, before a large chunk of door frame was ripped from where my head had been a split second before by a load of buckshot fired from behind an opened door.

Motioning for Marie to move out of the way, I snapped off three fast shots at the wall I figured my attacker was hiding behind and was rewarded with the sound of a body hitting the floor in the next room. I figured that at least one of my bullets had found its mark.

Then, down the hall, I heard more gunfire and the sound of running feet as a stranger dressed in the clothes of a cowboy ran into Marie's room with his pistol drawn and firing down the hall at someone. I didn't know if he was friend or foe, but I wasn't in the mood to take any chances, so drawing back the hammer, I pointed my pistol at him and, said, "Drop the gun or be dropped."

While I was unsure as to whether or not this man was my enemy, he had no such problem. Whirling around he dropped into a crouch preparing to fire and Marie and I both shot him.

Walking cautiously to the body, I rolled it out into the hallway. Carefully, I stepped out into the smoke-filled hall. And while the smoke was still thick, I could see well enough to notice that all of the doors had been kicked in. Checking the room to my right, I saw that the man with the shotgun was down with three tightly grouped bullet holes in his chest.

Not knowing if I had any allies left, I took a chance and yelled out, "This is Matt Coltrane. Anybody who's on my side and still able to talk, sing out!"

A few seconds later, Shorty answered, "I reckon I'm the

only one, Matt. And I've got some buckshot in me and can't stand. I guess you're on your own."

Reaching over I touched the Pinkerton's neck in search of a pulse, and felt only cold clammy skin. It was obvious that he had been dead for some time. I had no doubt that the guard in the lobby had met the same fate. Walking on down the hall to the other Pinkerton's room I found three dead guards and one cowpoke. Continuing on to Shorty's room, I sang out, "It's Matt, don't shoot!"

Hearing him lower the hammer on his pistol, I walked on into the room. Shorty was on the floor, leaning against the wall where he had made his bed. His right leg was bleeding and I could see where the shotgun pellets had entered below his knee. Walking over to the bed, I tore a piece of bed sheet and used it to bandage his damaged leg. "That'll stop the bleeding until I can get a doctor up here," I said, tying off the makeshift tourniquet."

"I got two of 'em," Shorty said. "One broke through my door with a shotgun and blew apart the pillow I stuck under my sheet," he said, pointing to the hole in the bed and the feathers scattered all over the room. "I had been sleeping pretty heavy and if he hadn't of fired both barrels of his shotgun and been forced to try for his pistol, I doubt that I would have been fast enough to win the drawing contest I had with him. And like I said, being a little slow this morning it was a while until I got to the door and met the men who had shot the Pinkertons coming out of their room. I think we were all surprised when we met. But I did manage to get one of them before the second one got me in the leg with a load of buckshot. After that I crawled back into my room and we traded shots in the hall until he ran into your room. I figure you took care of him?"

Nodding, I said, "Well, Marie and I did. In fact, of the four I got, Marie helped with three of them."

"Good girl," he said. "There's a lot to that one."

"Coltrane! Matt Coltrane!" said a voice from the lobby.

The hair on the back of my neck stood up and I felt as if I had just woke up with a rattlesnake buzzing next to my ear.

"Mr. Coltrane, my name is Laborteaux, and I believe that we have the opportunity to solve our dispute permanently. Come on down and let us be gentlemen about this matter."

Shucking the empties from both of my Colts, I loaded every chamber.

Once again, the voice drifted up from the lobby, "I am going out into the street now, Mr. Coltrane. You can come out at your leisure. You don't have to worry about anybody shooting you in the back, since you've killed all of my men. It's a shame though. Jacques and Pierre were two of the best assassins in the business. They had never failed me until now. Of course, the others were just local talent and apparently not even worth the few dollars I paid them."

I heard his steps as he walked to the door and opened it. "I'll be waiting, my friend," he said, and walked out the door.

Shorty grabbed my arm and said, "Don't do it, Matt. He's either better with a gun than you are or he's got some kind of an ambush set for you."

"I doubt that he's got any men left. I think he used everybody he had in one big push and figured to overwhelm us with numbers. And he almost did. But it doesn't matter. I don't have any choice. I have to kill him or die trying. And I'd rather face him out in the open, than wonder where he was and what he was plotting for the rest of my and Marie's lives."

Shorty sighed. "I guess you're right, Matt."

"Something else you need to think about. I'm going to do my best to put lead into him, but if he wins, you need to figure out some way of killing him, because he will certainly kill you and Marie if you don't."

"I agree," said Shorty.

"One other matter, and I find having to say it as distasteful as you will hearing it. It concerns Marie's aunt. Marie can hire all of the guards she wants to, but her aunt will never give up trying to get her killed. And you too since I know that you are stubborn enough to try and prevent it."

"What are you trying to say, Matt?"

"I'm trying to say that as soon as you're able you need to set out and kill that woman."

"I know that you're right, Matt, but that will be a very hard thing for me to do."

"I know. I'm not even sure I could do it myself," I said, walking to the door.

"Marie," I yelled into the hallway.

Marie came out of the doorway with her derringer in front of her.

"Marie, I have to go down and face your uncle in the street. If I don't make it back, stay up here with Shorty. Sooner or later some of the good people in this town will come up here and help you. As soon as possible hire new bodyguards, and contact Rink and let him know what has happened and then head for someplace safe, if you can find such a place."

Seeing the tears starting to well up in her eyes, I reached over to kiss her for what I figured could very well be the last time.

I was walking down a flight of stairs, but I felt more like I was walking up the steps of a gallows to a waiting hangman's noose.

I had returned to my room to retrieve my coat and cane and once at the bottom of the stairs, I began walking using the cane in my left hand. Laborteaux had left the door open, so I walked straight on out into the street to meet him. He wore the same black broad cloth suit he had on before and had pulled back the skirt of his coat to expose the pearl handled Smith & Wesson he wore low and tied down. Walking to within fifty feet of him, I said, "I'm here. Let's get to it."

He looked amused. "Get right to the point, don't you, boy?" He said holding out his hands far away from the pistol at his side. "But I like to talk to a man before I kill him."

As he spoke I noticed that he was gradually bringing his right hand to bear on me. Looking closely, I could see the muzzles of the derringer. Fortunately, I had been taught that lesson before and I had decided to use a trick of my own design. Letting go of the cane, it fell to the ground and Laborteaux's eyes followed it. That gave me the edge I needed. Crouching, I leaned to my right, drew, and fired a split second before he realized that he had been tricked.

Walking over to him, I looked into his eyes and could see that he was dead. With a great deal of relief, I dropped the Colt back into the holster and started back for the hotel. I had gone about ten feet when I heard a feminine voice say, "Turn around, Mr. Coltrane."

Turning around slowly, I saw Marie's aunt pointing the muzzle of a .45 Colt between my eyes. "My brother had a sense of fair play that I'm not burdened with," she said as she started to squeeze the trigger.

As I stood there rooted to the ground waiting for the gun to go off, I wondered how it was that Marie's aunt could think of her brother shooting me with a hide-out gun as fair play. When I heard the shot, it sounded familiar—a sound that I'd heard many times before. It had the same sharp bark that my old squirrel rifle had, and it seemed like it had been fired from somewhere behind me. It was then that I noticed that a small blue hole had appeared on Marie's aunt's forehead. The pistol dropped from her hand and she slumped to the sidewalk.

Turning around, I saw Marie standing in front of the hotel with the smoking squirrel rifle tightly gripped in her hands. Dropping the gun, she ran over to me, threw her arms around my waist, and hugged me so hard that I almost passed out from the pressure she was putting on my wounds.

Walking back to the hotel, I stopped and looked up the street.

"What's the matter?" she asked, "Are there more of them?"

"No. Just looking for a church," I said.

"Why?"

Taking her by the arm, I said, " 'Cause we need to find us a preacher."

The next day we got word from Marie's attorney that a decision had been reached concerning her rights to her inheritance. The court had ruled that Marie was entitled to a one-third share of the proceeds from the silver mine in Nevada and all properties bought with the proceeds from said mine.

And since Marie was the only living relative of the late Leon Laborteaux, she was now the sole owner of the mine and everything that her aunt and uncle had bought with the silver taken from it. That included the fine mansion that they had invited her to in hopes of killing her. Now, with the sale of my cattle and all, I wasn't exactly what you could have called a pauper, but I was feeling a might touchy about my future wife having so much money that she could buy and sell me several times over. But every time that I saw her smile, my thoughts along those lines melted away faster than ice in July.

A month later everybody who was close to us—that being friends and the like since we were both fresh out of blood kin—gathered at what was soon to be our mansion in New Orleans for the type of wedding that neither of us had ever dreamed of attending, let alone being the center of attention at.

Shorty was there acting as my best man while supporting himself on a crutch and propping himself up against whatever he could find handy. Mrs. Warren had been Marie's choice for maid of honor, and even John Rink had shown up to give the bride away, but he spent most of his time prowling about the mansion trying to talk me and Shorty into coming to work for him transporting jewels through some Asian country where he said the pay would be top rate and there was a good chance that we'd all get rich if we didn't get killed first. I'd pretty much convinced him that I was going to give married life a try—since I was going to the trouble of having a wedding and all, but I could see that Shorty was weakening and that as soon as his legs were healed he would be following Rink off on some job that would pay him well and require him to risk his life on a regular basis.

But I had decided to try the quiet life—at least for the time being. And when the preacher got to the part in the vows where he asked Marie about whether or not she was willing to take me for better or worse, I was sure that I had made the right decision when I heard her say, "Always have—always will."